PUFFIN BOOKS

THE PUFFIN BOOK OF ANIMAL STORIES

Never were there so many fascinating, funny, like-able animal characters from all corners of the globe as clever Elephant Little who taught Elephant Big how much better brains were than brawn, kind Koala who stopped his expedition so many times to help other animals, poor old Quail who could never make up his mind, and the small Gorilla who refused to eat his carrots. All the tales are told with a sparkling sense of fun, and more than a grain of true information about the animals rubs off in the process.

Anita Hewett is one of those authors who know exactly the sort of story that appeals to young children. Because she worked as a kindergarten teacher, ran her own school, and worked for some years in the Schools Broadcasting Department of the BBC, she has a unique understanding of how to write a story that is going to be read aloud, which is why the thirty-five stories in this book are so superb for reading aloud to children of five or six, and stimulating enough to make the new reader persevere.

ANITA HEWETT

The Puffin Book of
Animal Stories

ILLUSTRATED BY
MARGERY GILL AND
CHARLOTTE HOUGH

Puffin Books

in association with The Bodley Head

PUFFIN BOOKS

Penguin Books Ltd, 27 Wrights Lane, London w8 5TZ (Publishing and Editorial)
and Harmondsworth, Middlesex, England (Distribution and Warehouse)
Viking Penguin Inc., 40 West 23rd Street, New York, New York 10010, USA
Penguin Books Australia Ltd, Ringwood, Victoria, Australia
Penguin Books Canada Ltd, 2801 John Street, Markham, Ontario, Canada L3R 1B4
Penguin Books (NZ) Ltd, 182–190 Wairau Road, Auckland 10, New Zealand

Chapters 1–9 were first published as *Elephant Big and Elephant Little* in 1955;
chapters 10–19 were first published as *Honey Mouse* in 1957;
chapters 20–26 were first published as *The Little Yellow Jungle Frogs* in 1956;
and chapters 27–35 were first published as *A Hat for Rhinoceros* in 1959

First published as *The Anita Hewett Animal Story Book* by The Bodley Head 1972
Published in Puffin Books 1974
Reprinted 1975, 1977, 1980, 1984
Reissued as *The Puffin Book of Animal Stories*, 1988

This collection © Anita Hewett, 1972
Illustrations © The Bodley Head Ltd, 1972
All rights reserved

Made and printed in Great Britain by
Richard Clay Ltd, Bungay, Suffolk

Contents

Stories of African Animals

Stories of Australian Animals

Stories of South American Animals

Stories of South-East Asian Animals

Stories of
African Animals

illustrated by Charlotte Hough

The Jackal that Teased

NAUGHTY Jackal ran through the forest, looking for someone to tease. When he saw Antelope, he hid.

'Antelope runs so fast,' he said. 'He would certainly catch me and spank me hard.' Then he met Beetle.

'Oho!' he chuckled. 'Here's someone to tease.'

He put out his tongue in a very rude fashion, and called:

'Silly Beetle! Hoddydoddy! He he he!
·Beetle's small! Beetle's small and can't catch me.'

Beetle was so annoyed that she buzzed.

'Naughty Jackal! Naughty Jackal!' she scolded. 'You need a good spanking.' But being so small, she could not catch him.

On through the forest Jackal ran, looking for someone to tease. When he saw Leopard, he hid. 'Leopard is much too big,' he said. 'He would certainly catch me and spank me hard.' Then he met Pig.

'Oho!' he chuckled. 'Here's someone to tease.' He put out his tongue in a very rude fashion, and called:

'Silly Pig! Hoddydoddy! He he he!
Pig is fat! Pig is fat and can't catch me.'

Pig was so annoyed that he squealed.

'Naughty Jackal! Naughty Jackal!' he scolded. 'You need a good spanking.' But being so fat, he could not catch him.

On through the forest Jackal ran, looking for someone to tease. When he saw Jumping Hare, he hid.

'Hare can jump too fast,' he said. 'He would certainly catch me and spank me hard.' Then he met Porcupine.

'Oho!' he chuckled. 'Here's someone to tease.' He put out his tongue in a very rude fashion, and called:

'Silly Porky! Hoddydoddy! He he he!
Porcupine has short legs and can't catch me.'

Porcupine was so annoyed that he rattled his quills.

'Naughty Jackal! Naughty Jackal!' he scolded. But his legs being so short, he could not catch him.

'Well really!' he said. 'Jackal will have to be caught and spanked. I will go and see Lion.'

Porcupine hurried to Lion's den, to find Beetle and Pig already there.

'That Jackal is naughty,' buzzed Beetle.

'He will have to be caught,' squealed Pig.

'And spanked!' added Porcupine, rattling his quills.

'H'm!' grunted Lion. 'Jackal is cunning. *I* could catch him of course. So could Antelope, Leopard, or Jumping Hare. But not if he sees us first! I must think.'

As Lion lay in his den, thinking, he looked up and noticed Giraffe. Giraffe was eating some fresh green leaves that grew at the top of a tall tree. Lion looked at Giraffe's long neck and made his plan.

'Follow me, Beetle, Pig, and Porcupine,' he said. 'Giraffe must come too. We are going to the high fence that stands by the forest road.'

Lion set off at once for the road, with Giraffe, Beetle, Pig, and Porcupine stepping smartly along behind him. On the way they were joined by Antelope, Leopard, and Jumping Hare.

'Now, behind that high fence, all of you!' Lion ordered, when they reached the road.

Behind the fence was a path. Lion, Antelope, Leopard, Jumping Hare, and Giraffe stood in line on the path. Beetle, Pig, and Porcupine peeped out at the road through three small holes in the fence.

'Now, are you ready?' asked Lion. 'Quick march!'

Lion, Antelope, Leopard, Jumping Hare, and Giraffe marched up the path behind the fence.

'About turn!' Lion shouted, and they all turned around and marched *down* the path. They marched up and down, and up and down, but all you could see from the road on the other side of the fence was tall Giraffe's head and the upper part of his long neck. Up and down, up and down, marched Lion, Antelope, Leopard, Jumping Hare, and Giraffe.

Presently Beetle nudged Pig, and Pig whispered to Porcupine: 'Jackal! Look! Jackal is coming. He's coming along the road.'

Jackal stopped and stared when he came to the fence. All he could see was tall Giraffe's head and the upper part of his long neck. He grinned all over his face as he said: 'Why are you marching up and down, up and down, all by yourself behind that high fence?'

Giraffe looked up at the sky, and sighed. 'I like to
march by myself,' he said. Beetle, Pig, and Porcupine
covered their mouths to stop themselves from laughing out loud.

'Oho!' thought Jackal. 'Silly Giraffe will be easy
to tease. He can't jump over that high fence and catch
me.'

He put out his tongue in a very rude fashion, and
called:

'Silly Giraffe! Hoddydoddy! He he he!
Giraffe's behind a high fence and can't catch me.'

'Halt!' roared Lion. And –
'Leap!' roared Lion.
Antelope, Leopard, and Jumping Hare leapt lightly

and easily over the fence. They ran at squealing Jackal and caught him. Antelope held him and spanked him hard. Leopard held him and spanked him harder. Jumping Hare held him and spanked him hardest of all.

'Ee ee ee!' squealed naughty Jackal. 'I don't like being spanked.' And he squealed and squealed.

'We didn't like being teased,' said Beetle, Pig, and Porcupine. Then they danced with delight behind the high fence.

The Leopard that Lost a Spot

LEOPARD lay beneath a tree, carefully counting his spots. There were ninety-eight, sooty black on his soft yellow fur.

'Oh do stop counting your silly spots,' Monkey called from the branches above.

'Eighty-five, eighty-six, eighty-seven, eighty-eight,' counted Leopard.

'Silly Leopard!' Monkey said. 'I'm tired of hearing you counting all day.' And away he ran across the forest to the house where Man lived.

Man was painting a yellow fence, and Monkey watched from behind a thorn bush. When noon came and the sun grew hot, Man put down his pot of paint and went inside his house to rest. This was what Monkey had waited for! He snatched up the yellow paint and the brush, and scampered back across the forest to the tree where Leopard still counted his spots. He hid the paint in the long grass, climbed the tree, sat on a branch, and waited.

Leopard counted his spots once more. Then he said: 'They are all there. That is good. I will sleep.'

As soon as the Leopard began to snore, Monkey came quietly down the tree. He picked up the pot of yellow paint and tiptoed close to the leopard. He looked at Leopard's black spots very carefully, until he found the biggest of all. He dipped the brush in the yellow paint, and painted over that big black spot so that it did not show. Then he hid the paint in the grass, climbed up into the tree, sat on a branch, and waited.

When Leopard awoke he yawned three times. Then he started counting his spots.

'One, two, three,' he said, and counted up to ninety-seven.

'Only ninety-seven! Just ninety-seven!' he cried. 'I ought to have ninety-eight. I've lost a spot! Oh what shall I do? I've lost a spot!'

Monkey, on his branch above, laughed so much that he nearly choked.

17

'Where is my ninety-eighth spot?' cried Leopard. 'Where is it? Where is my spot?'

Then he looked wise.

'I expect I am sitting on it,' he said, and he stood up and snuffled about in the grass.

Monkey, on his branch above, laughed so much that his sides ached. Leopard ran off through the forest, calling: 'Where is my spot? I must find my spot.'

Porcupine looked for it, Elephant looked for it, Lion looked for it, Snake looked for it. They searched high and they searched low, but they could not find that missing spot. Then thunder rolled across the sky and drops of rain splashed on Leopard. Porcupine, Elephant, Lion, and Snake took shelter, but Leopard stayed out in the pouring rain because he was anxious to find his spot. When the storm passed and the sun shone, Leopard was tired and exceedingly wet.

'I will rest for a while beneath my tree, and the sun will dry my fur,' he said. Then a dreadful fear came into his mind. Perhaps he had lost another spot!

'One, two, three,' he said, and counted up to ninety-eight.

'Ninety-eight!' he cried in delight. 'It's come back again! My spot has come back! Now how could a spot get lost like that, and then find its own way back?'

Monkey, on his branch above, laughed so much that he nearly fell out of the tree. But he did not tell Leopard about the paint, or that the rain had washed if off so that the spot could show again.

'Strange!' said Leopard. 'Exceedingly strange!'

Then Monkey laughed and laughed so much that he really did fall out of the tree. He did not fall on the soft leaves. Nor did he fall in the long grass. He fell where he deserved to fall – in the pot of yellow paint!

Mr and Mrs Ostrich

'I AM going to lay some eggs,' said Mrs Ostrich.

'That is good,' Mr Ostrich smiled. 'When they hatch out into baby ostriches, we shall be proud of our fine family; but first you must make a nest to hold the eggs.'

'You are quite right,' Mrs Ostrich agreed. 'Now where shall I make it?'

Mr Ostrich ran about among the tall, dry grass, searching for a safe place.

'Here you are, my dear,' he said at last. 'I have found a patch of sandy earth among the grass.'

Mrs Ostrich stretched her long neck, and looked about her.

'It is not too near the river,' she said. 'So when Elephant and Lion come to drink at night they won't wake up my babies. But it's rather near the forest road. Man comes down the forest road. Will he see my eggs and steal them?'

'Man won't see the eggs,' smiled Mr Ostrich. 'And even if he did, he wouldn't steal them.'

'A family means a lot of worry,' Mrs Ostrich sighed. 'But I mustn't think too much about the dangers. I must make the nest.'

She sat down on the soft sandy earth, and turned around and around and around until she had scooped out a hollow nest.

'Now I must flatten the edges with my wings,' she said. 'And now the nest is finished.'

Then Mrs Ostrich laid twelve eggs.

'We must sit on the eggs to keep them warm until they hatch,' said Mr Ostrich. 'I will sit on them every night.'

'And I will sit on them every day,' smiled Mrs Ostrich.

All went well, until one day Man walked down the forest road.

'I am sure he'll steal my eggs,' cried Mrs Ostrich.

'Nonsense my dear!' Mr Ostrich said. 'He's much too busy lighting up his pipe. Ah! Now it's alight, and look, my dear, he's waving to us.'

Man was not really waving to the ostriches. He was shaking a burning match in order to put out the flame. He threw down the match and walked on along the road. But the flame was not out. It flickered and began to burn the grass.

'Do you hear that crackling sound, my dear?' asked Mr Ostrich.

Mrs Ostrich stretched her long neck and looked about her.

'It's fire!' she cried. 'The grass is burning. The wind is blowing the fire towards our nest. All our babies will be burned inside their shells.'

'No! No!' cried Mr Ostrich. 'We must stop the fire.

Man beats out fire with sticks. We must use our feet to beat it down until we kill it.'

'Too late! Too late!' cried Mrs Ostrich. 'By the time we've killed the fire, my eggs will have become so hot that all my babies will be dead.'

Mr Ostrich ran towards the river, calling: 'Come, my dear, come quickly to the river.'

Mr and Mrs Ostrich splashed their wings in the sparkling river until their feathers dripped with water.

'Back to the nest!' cried Mr Ostrich. 'Run fast! Run fast to save our babies.'

When Mr and Mrs Ostrich reached the nest they stood beside it, beating their wet-feathered wings strongly up and down. Icy drops of river water spattered on the eggs to cool them.

Then Mr and Mrs Ostrich stamped and stamped the crackling, angry flames, thrashing down the fire until at last it died.

'And now, my dear, you need some rest,' said Mr Ostrich. 'You were very brave.'

'I do feel tired,' sighed Mrs Ostrich. 'But it doesn't matter. How could it matter now that we have saved our babies?'

'Listen!' whispered Mr Ostrich. 'Do you hear that tapping sound, my dear?'

Mrs Ostrich bent her long neck towards the eggs.

'Our babies have strong beaks,' she smiled. 'They are pecking at the shells.'

Then, one by one, twelve little baby ostriches came wriggling out of their shells.

'I feel so proud,' said Mr Ostrich.

'I feel so happy,' said Mrs Ostrich. 'There cannot be babies stronger or more beautiful than ours.'

The Saucepan Fish

'Now this is a funny thing,' said Monkey.

He stood beside the forest road, looking down at the strange round shining thing that lay quite still on the grass.

Man had just driven his rattly old car down the road, and this Thing had suddenly tumbled out of the luggage boot at the back. It made no sound as it fell on the grass, so Man did not know he had lost his new saucepan.

'I wonder if it's alive,' said Monkey. 'It doesn't have

fur or feathers or hair, but it does seem to have a tail.'

He patted the saucepan gently and said: 'Hello, Thing. What's your name?'

After waiting to see if the saucepan would answer, he scratched his head and said to himself: 'I'll pull its tail and see if it squeaks.' He seized the saucepan handle and pulled. 'No, it doesn't squeak; it can't be alive. I'll see if Porcupine knows what it is.'

Porcupine was asleep in his burrow. He grunted crossly when Monkey awakened him, then peered at the saucepan with sleepy eyes.

'Of course it's not alive,' he said. 'It's a seat. Man sits on a seat, instead of on the ground as we do.'

Then he closed his eyes and slept again.

'A seat!' said Monkey. 'So that's what it is.' He turned the saucepan upside down, and sat on it; then he put a grass stalk in his mouth and made puffing noises.

'I'm Man, smoking a pipe,' he chuckled. 'It's a wonderful seat I have here, and I'm sure that Jay would like to see it.'

Jay was smoothing her bright feathers. She looked at the shiny saucepan and piped: 'It's not a seat at all, silly Monkey. That Thing is a mirror. Man looks in a mirror to see himself, instead of looking into the lake as we do.'

'A mirror!' said Monkey. 'So that's what it is.' He propped the saucepan against a tree trunk, and laughed to see his own brown face. Then he patted his head with his paws.

'I'm Man, brushing my hair,' he chuckled. 'It's a

wonderful mirror I have, and I'm sure that Pig would like to see it.'

Pig was rooting. He looked at the shiny saucepan and grunted: 'It's not a mirror at all, silly Monkey. It's a hat. Man puts a hat on his head, instead of just wearing hair as we do.'

'A hat!' said Monkey. 'So that's what it is.'

He fitted the saucepan over his head, with the handle sticking out at the back. It was so big that it covered his face and rested on his shoulders.

'Oh dear!' he grumbled. 'It's dark in here, and I can't see where I'm going.' He took the saucepan off his head, and knocked two holes in its side with a sharp stone. When he put the saucepan back on his head, his two bright eyes peered through the holes.

'That's better,' he chuckled, marching smartly along the path. 'I'm Man, going for a walk. It's a wonderful hat that I have, and I'm sure that Frog would like to see it.'

Frog was on the river bank, chasing gnats. When he saw the saucepan marching towards him, with Monkey's body and legs beneath it, he croaked in terror and hopped away.

'It's only me,' Monkey called him back. 'It's only me, and I've found a hat.'

Frog came closer. His eyes bulged as he stared at the saucepan hat. Then he said: 'It's not a hat at all, silly Monkey. It's a boat. Man floats on the river in it, instead of swimming as we do.'

'*I* can't swim,' Monkey told him.

'Then sit in the boat, as Man does,' said Frog.

Monkey sat in the saucepan boat, and Frog pushed it into the river. For a minute it floated. Then water poured in through the holes. With a splash and a gurgle it sank.

'Help!' yelled Monkey, thrashing his legs in the icy water. 'Help! Help! My boat has sunk!'

A big dark shape swam up beneath him. Hippopotamus appeared. 'Climb on my back,' said the kindly creature. 'I'll carry you back to the bank.'

When Monkey was drying himself in the sunshine, he said: 'Thank you, Hippopotamus. Thank you for rescuing me when my boat sank.'

Hippopotamus looked at him kindly. 'You are really a silly little Monkey,' he said. 'That wasn't a boat at all.'

'What was it?' asked Monkey and Frog together.

'A fish, of course!' Hippopotamus smiled.

'A fish!' cried Monkey. 'What would Man want with a fish?'

But Hippopotamus was back in the river, blowing little popping bubbles, and he would not answer.

'A fish!' said Monkey. 'Well, I can't see it now, and that seems to mean that it swam away.'

'It did have a tail,' said Frog. 'Yes, indeed, it could be a fish.'

Frog and Monkey looked at each other and nodded wisely.

'Hippopotamus is old,' said Frog.

'Hippopotamus is wise,' said Monkey.

'Hippopotamus is right,' they said together. 'Of course it must have been a fish.'

Chameleons Never Laugh

Two little lion cubs were playing 'tag'.

'I'll catch you!' cried Nippy.

'You won't!' shouted Skippy.

'I can't rest for the noise you're making,' said Mother Lion. 'Off you go to the long grass, and practise stalking, like good cubs.'

'Yes, Mother,' said Nippy and Skippy, and off they ran to the long grass. First, they practised stalking a tree. They crouched low in the long grass and crept forward without a sound. Then they swung their tails and sprang at the tree.

'We caught it!' cried Nippy. 'It didn't see us.'

'Of course it didn't,' Skippy snorted. 'Trees can't see; they haven't got eyes.'

'Let's try stalking an anthill,' said Nippy.

31

'Neither can anthills see,' said Skippy, turning up his little black nose. 'It's no fun stalking things that can't see. Let's stalk Chameleon.'

Nippy looked frightened.

'But Chameleon's so bad-tempered,' he said. 'He'll be ever so angry.'

'I know,' chuckled Skippy. 'And when he gets angry he goes all spotty, and then he turns green, or yellow, or black. He looks so funny he makes me laugh. Come on, Nippy. Let's go and stalk him.'

Chameleon sat at the top of a thorn bush. His small body was quite still, until all of a sudden he puffed his cheeks and darted out his long, narrow tongue.

'He's catching insects,' Nippy whispered. 'And he's looking dreadfully cross about it.'

'Chameleon never laughs,' said Skippy. 'But we shall laugh when we stalk him and catch him.'

The lion cubs crouched in the long grass, and crept towards the thorn bush. They made no sound and the long grass hid them. Nearer and nearer and nearer they crept. Then they swung their tails, and Chameleon saw them. How angry he was! He snapped at the air and grunted with anger. Then Nippy and Skippy laughed and laughed, for Chameleon's skin went spotty all over. He turned green with anger, then yellow with anger, then black with anger. Nippy and Skippy rolled on the ground and laughed till the tears ran down their whiskers.

'Be off, naughty cubs!' Chameleon scolded. 'Be off with you, before I bite you.'

Nippy and Skippy scampered away, and hid themselves behind an anthill.

'He did look funny,' Nippy laughed. 'I'd like to see him do it again.'

'You will,' said Skippy. 'We'll stalk him again, and this time we'll catch him.'

Nippy's eyes grew round as buttons.

'But we can't,' he said. 'He'll be watching for us. He'll see us before we get anywhere near him.'

'He won't,' chuckled Skippy. 'We'll stalk him from two ways at once. I can stalk him from in front, and you can stalk him from behind. Then one of us is sure to catch him. He can't look behind and in front at the same time.'

Nippy put his paw to his mouth to stop himself from laughing out loud.

'We must keep very quiet,' Skippy told him. 'But when we've caught him, we'll laugh and laugh.'

'Chameleon won't laugh,' said Nippy.

'Chameleon never laughs,' said Skippy.

Nippy walked in half a circle and reached a spot behind the thorn bush. Skippy stayed in front of the thorn bush. Then both cubs crouched low in the long grass and crept towards Chameleon. They made no sound and the long grass hid them. Chameleon sat quite still on the thorn bush. Nippy and Skippy crept nearer and nearer.

'He can't watch us both at once,' thought Nippy. 'If he looks forward, he can't look backward.'

'He won't see both of us spring,' thought Skippy. 'If he looks backward he can't look forward.'

33

Closer and closer the lion cubs crept, until they were near enough to spring. Two tufted tails swung from side to side, and two pairs of eyes shone bright with laughter. Then Nippy sprang, from behind the thorn bush, and Skippy sprang, from in front of the thorn bush. Chameleon darted down to the ground, and the heads of the lion cubs met with a bump! Two sad little cubs tumbled down in a heap, looking very surprised. They sat on the grass and rubbed their sore heads, and could not think what had become of Chameleon.

Chameleon sat on top of the anthill. His little grey body was shaking with laughter.

'Clever little lion cubs! Brave little lion cubs!' he teased them. 'Thought you could catch Chameleon, eh? Cubs didn't know that Chameleon looks two ways at once. He can look forward with one eye, and backward with the other eye.'

Chameleon held his little grey sides because he was laughing so much that they ached.

'Chameleon never laughs!' he chuckled. 'Ah ha! He he! But he's laughing now, and he's laughing at you, looking so funny sitting there, blinking your eyes and rubbing your heads. Chameleon never laughs. Ah ha! Chameleon never laughs. He he!'

He jumped up and down on top of the anthill, laughing as though he would burst.

Nippy and Skippy ran home to their mother.

'So Chameleon laughed!' smiled Mother Lion. 'And why did he laugh?'

'He laughed at us,' said Nippy and Skippy. Then

each little lion cub tried very hard to look forward with one eye and backward with the other.

And far away, on top of his thorn bush, Chameleon laughed and laughed and laughed.

Elephant Big and Elephant Little

ELEPHANT BIG was always boasting.

'I'm bigger and better than you,' he told Elephant Little. 'I can run faster, and shoot water higher out of my trunk, and eat more, and . . .'

'No. You can't!' said Elephant Little.

Elephant Big was surprised. Elephant Big was *always* right. Then he curled up his trunk and laughed and laughed.

'What's more, I'll show you,' said Elephant Little. 'Let's have a running race, and a shooting-water-out-of-our-trunks race, and an eating race. We'll soon see who wins.'

'I shall, of course,' boasted Elephant Big. 'Lion shall be judge.'

'The running race first!' Lion said. 'Run two miles there and two miles back. One of you runs in the field, the other one runs in the forest. Elephant Big shall choose.'

Elephant Big thought and thought, and Elephant Little pretended to talk to himself: 'I hope he chooses to run in the field, because *I* want to run in the forest.'

When Elephant Big heard this, he thought: 'If Elephant Little wants very much to run in the forest, that means the forest is best.' Aloud he said: 'I choose the forest.'

'Very well,' said Lion. 'One, two, three. Go!'

Elephant Little had short legs, but they ran very fast on the springy smooth grass of the field. Elephant Big had long, strong legs, but they could not carry him quickly along through the forest. Broken branches lay in his way; thorns tore at him; tangled grass caught at his feet. By the time he stumbled, tired and panting, back to the winning post, Elephant Little had run his four miles, and was standing talking to Lion.

'What ages you've been!' said Elephant Little. 'We thought you were lost.'

'Elephant Little wins,' said Lion.

Elephant Little smiled to himself.

'But I'll win the next race,' said Elephant Big. 'I can shoot water much higher than you can.'

'All right!' said Lion. 'One of you fills his trunk

from the river, the other fills his trunk from the lake. Elephant Big shall choose.'

Elephant Big thought and thought, and Elephant Little pretended to talk to himself: 'I hope he chooses the river, because *I* want to fill my trunk from the lake.'

When Elephant Big heard this, he thought: 'If Elephant Little wants very much to fill his trunk from the lake, that means the lake is best.' Aloud he said: 'I choose the lake.'

'Very well!' said Lion. 'One, two, three. Go!'

Elephant Little ran to the river and filled his trunk with clear, sparkling water. His trunk was small, but he spouted the water as high as a tree.

Elephant Big ran to the lake, and filled his long, strong trunk with water. But the lake water was heavy with mud, and full of slippery, tickly fishes. When Elephant Big spouted it out, it rose only as high as a middle-sized thorn bush. He lifted his trunk and tried harder than ever. A cold little fish slipped down his throat, and Elephant Big spluttered and choked.

'Elephant Little wins,' said Lion.

Elephant Little smiled to himself.

When Elephant Big stopped coughing, he said: 'But I'll win the next race, see if I don't. I can eat much more than you can.'

'Very well!' said Lion. 'Eat where you like and how you like.'

Elephant Big thought and thought, and Elephant Little pretended to talk to himself: 'I must eat and

eat as fast as I can, and I mustn't stop; not for a minute.'

Elephant Big thought to himself: 'Then I must do exactly the same. I must eat and eat as fast as I can, and I mustn't stop; not for a minute.'

'Are you ready?' asked Lion. 'One, two, three. Go!'

Elephant Big bit and swallowed, and bit and swallowed, as fast as he could, without stopping. Before very long, he began to feel full up inside.

Elephant Little bit and swallowed, and bit and swallowed. Then he stopped eating and ran round a thorn bush three times. He felt perfectly well inside.

Elephant Big went on biting and swallowing, biting

and swallowing, without stopping. He began to feel very, very funny inside.

Elephant Little bit and swallowed, and bit and swallowed. Then again he stopped eating, and ran round a thorn bush six times. He felt perfectly well inside.

Elephant Big bit and swallowed, and bit and swallowed, as fast as he could, without stopping once, until he felt so dreadfully ill inside that he had to sit down.

Elephant Little had just finished running around a thorn bush nine times, and he still felt perfectly well inside. When he saw Elephant Big on the ground, holding his tummy and groaning horribly, Elephant Little smiled to himself.

'Oh, I do like eating, don't you?' he said. 'I've only just started. I could eat and eat and eat and eat.'

'Oh, oh, oh!' groaned Elephant Big.

'Why, what's the matter?' asked Elephant Little. 'You look queer. Sort of green! When are you going to start eating again?'

'Not a single leaf more!' groaned Elephant Big. 'Not a blade of grass, not a twig can I eat!'

'Elephant Little wins,' said Lion.

Elephant Big felt too ill to speak.

After that day, if Elephant Big began to boast, Elephant Little smiled, and said: 'Shall we have a running race? Shall we spout water? Or shall we just eat and eat and eat?'

Then Elephant Big would remember. Before very long, he was one of the nicest, most friendly elephants ever to take a mud bath.

Small Gorilla and the Parsley

'Now eat up your carrot at once,' scolded Mother Gorilla.

'Shan't! Don't want it!' said Small Gorilla. 'Tired of carrot! Want parsley instead.'

'Now please,' his mother began to plead, but Father Gorilla frowned as he said: 'If Small Gorilla is too fussy to eat his carrot, let him set out to find his own parsley. In any case, it is time that he learnt to look after himself.'

Small Gorilla threw down his carrot and scampered away.

'Parsley, fresh parsley!' he sang to himself, as he ran past the prickling thorn trees that grew near his home. 'O fresh, O green, O juicy parsley!'

He looked in the tufty grass for parsley; he looked among the sweet potatoes; he searched here and he searched there, but not one leaf could he find.

'I'm hungry,' he said. 'Enormously hungry! Oh look! There's Baboon, and he's eating his dinner.'

Baboon was eating a prickly pear.

'I suppose you wouldn't have seen any parsley,' sighed Small Gorilla.

'Parsley!' said the Big Baboon. 'What's parsley? *I* eat prickly pears for dinner. There, you can have one.'

'Oh kind Baboon!' cried Small Gorilla. He took a big bite of the prickly pear, and squealed with pain as its sharp little spines scratched his mouth.

'Silly Gorilla!' Baboon scolded. 'You ought to have rubbed it hard on the ground.' And he rubbed the prickly pear on the ground to scrape off the spines.

'I'll do that next time,' said Small Gorilla, as he set off once more to look for his dinner. 'Though I'd rather eat parsley, of course.'

He looked among the rocks for parsley; he looked in the ditch beside the road; he searched here and he searched there, but not one leaf could he find.

'I'm hungry,' he said. 'Enormously, dreadfully hungry! Why, there's Secretary Bird, and he's eating his dinner.'

Secretary Bird was eating a snake.

'I suppose you wouldn't have seen any parsley,' sighed Small Gorilla.

'Parsley!' said Secretary Bird. 'What's parsley? *I* eat snakes for my dinner. There, you can have one.'

Small Gorilla remembered the prickly pear. He held the wriggling snake in his paw, and rubbed it hard on the ground. The snake darted its head upwards and bit Small Gorilla, right on his nose.

'Ee ee ee!' squealed Small Gorilla.

'Silly creature!' scolded Secretary Bird. 'You ought to have jumped on the snake.' He lifted his long thin legs off the ground, and thud! he jumped on the snake and killed it.

'I'll do that next time,' said Small Gorilla, as he

set off once more to look for his dinner. 'Though I'd
rather have parsley, of course.'

He looked beneath the palm trees for parsley; he
looked in the empty water holes; he searched here
and he searched there, but not one leaf could he
find.

'I'm hungry,' he said. 'Enormously, dreadfully, terribly hungry! Oh, there's Hyena, eating his dinner.'

Hyena was eating an ostrich egg.

'I suppose you wouldn't have seen any parsley,'
sighed Small Gorilla.

'Parsley!' said Hyena. 'What's parsley? *I* eat
ostrich eggs for my dinner. There, you can have one.'

Small Gorilla remembered the snake. He lifted all
four legs off the ground, and thud! he jumped on the
ostrich egg, smashing it into a sticky mess.

'Silly creature!' Hyena scolded. 'You ought to have

tapped the egg with a stone.' He tapped an egg with a sharp little stone, and made a small hole.

'I'll do that next time,' said Small Gorilla. 'Though I'd rather eat parsley, of course.'

He looked in the wet muddy ground for parsley; he looked beside the wide green river; he searched here and he searched there, but not one leaf could he find.

'I'm hungry,' he said. 'Enormously, dreadfully, terribly, horribly hungry. Ah! There's Chameleon, eating his dinner.'

Chameleon was catching gnats.

'I suppose you wouldn't have seen any parsley,' sighed Small Gorilla.

'Parsley!' said Chameleon. 'What's parsley? *I* eat gnats for my dinner. There's one! It's flying over my head. You can have it.'

Small Gorilla remembered the ostrich egg.

'But I can't tap that gnat with a stone,' he said. 'It won't keep still. I must throw the stone.' He picked up a sharp little stone, and threw it, but the gnat flew away, and the stone hit Chameleon.

Chameleon danced and screamed with rage, and Small Gorilla fled in terror, pushing through the tangled grass and hurting himself on the prickly bushes. He ran and ran, gasping for breath, until he was aching and sore all over, and crying so much that he could not see where he was going.

'I'm hungry,' he moaned. 'I'm trembly with hunger.'

But when he wiped away his tears, he thought at first that he must be dreaming. For there, quite close to him, were the prickling thorn trees that grew near his home.

'Home! I'm home!' breathed Small Gorilla. 'I suppose there wouldn't be one little carrot; just one little carrot left over from dinner. Even a tough one would do.'

But Small Gorilla was not to eat carrot that day for his dinner. For he heard, from behind the prickling thorn trees, the good sound of gentle chewing. He crept to the trees and peeped around them, then rubbed his eyes and stared and stared. For there, on

48

the other side of the trees, grew fresh, green, juicy parsley. And among the parsley, eating their dinner, were Mother and Father Gorilla.

Small Gorilla walked slowly towards them, hanging his head. They smiled at him kindly.

'This is very good parsley,' said Mother Gorilla.

'Juicy parsley!' said Father Gorilla.

'Oh, it *is*! It *is*!' laughed Small Gorilla. Then beside the prickling thorn trees there was no more talking. There was only the gentle chewing sound of a small, happy gorilla eating his dinner!

A Piece of Yellow String

WART HOG and Rock Rabbit met in the forest.

'How silly you look!' said Wart Hog rudely. 'You have no tail at all.'

'*I* think I'm lucky,' Rabbit said crossly. 'I'd rather have no tail at all than the strange looking thing that you wear. It looks like a stick, with a tassel on the end.'

Wart Hog and Rock Rabbit frowned at each other.

'You have hurt my feelings,' Wart Hog grunted. 'Say you are sorry.'

'What about *my* feelings?' Rock Rabbit snorted. 'I won't say I'm sorry till you say it first.'

As Wart Hog and Rock Rabbit glared at each other, something fell on Wart Hog's head. It was only a piece of yellow string, but because it had seemed to fall from the sky, Wart Hog jumped, and squealed with fright.

'He he he!' Rock Rabbit giggled. 'Silly old Wart Hog! Wart Hog's afraid of a piece of string.'

The tuft of hair along Wart Hog's back stiffened with anger. He picked up the piece of yellow string and threw it at Rock Rabbit.

'Use it instead of a tail,' he shouted.

Rock Rabbit thumped his hind feet on the ground. Then he took the piece of yellow string and threw it back at Wart Hog.

'Use it to tie up your tassel,' he shouted.

Then Wart Hog threw the string at Rock Rabbit, and Rock Rabbit threw it back at Wart Hog, and Wart Hog threw it back at Rock Rabbit, and Rock Rabbit threw it back at Wart Hog.

'How dare you say that *I* need it!' squealed Wart Hog. 'Take it yourself.'

'How dare you say that I need it!' squealed Rock Rabbit. '*You* take it yourself.'

And so it went on and on and on, until Wart Hog had what he thought was a good idea. He threw the string and ran away, shouting: 'Now you'll have to keep it, so there! Because I'm going to hide behind a rock.' He hid behind a big black rock, but he quite forgot to hide his tusks. Rock Rabbit crept to those sticking-out tusks, and threw the string right over the rock, so that it landed on Wart Hog's back.

'Now *you'll* have to keep the string,' he shouted. 'Because I'm going to hide behind a bush.'

He hid behind a prickly bush, but he quite forgot to hide his ears.

Wart Hog peeped from behind his rock, then crept

towards those sticking-out ears. He threw the string right over the bush, so that it landed on Rock Rabbit's back.

'Now *you'll* have to keep the string,' he shouted. 'Because I'm going to hide behind an anthill.'

He hid behind a tall grey anthill, but he quite forgot to hide his tail.

Rock Rabbit peeped from behind his bush; then he crept towards that sticking-out tail, meaning to throw the string at Wart Hog. He and Wart Hog might still be throwing the string at each other to this day, had not Man come walking through the forest.

Wart Hog heard his heavy footsteps, and kept quite still behind the anthill. Rock Rabbit heard his footsteps too, and scampered back to the prickly thorn. In his haste, he dropped the piece of string, and left it on the forest path.

Man walked slowly along the path. He walked slowly because he had broken a bootlace. When he saw the piece of yellow string he stooped down and picked it up.

'What luck!' he thought. 'This piece of string will do for a bootlace, until I get home and find a real one.'

When Man had walked down the forest path with the yellow string laced up in his boot, Wart Hog peeped from behind his anthill.

'I don't see the string,' he said to himself. 'Rock Rabbit must have kept it. That means he's ready to say he's sorry, so I can say I'm sorry too.'

Rock Rabbit peeped from behind his bush.

'I don't see the string,' he said to himself. 'Wart Hog must have kept it. That means he's ready to say he's sorry, so I can say I'm sorry too.'

Wart Hog and Rock Rabbit met on the path.

They said to each other, both together:

'I'm sorry I spoke so rudely to you. Now let's be friends.'

Then Wart Hog and Rock Rabbit smiled at each other and walked side by side down the forest path.

The Garden

'A PRINCESS is coming to visit our country,' said Lion. 'Now how can we show her how happy we are to see her?'

'We could bow very low, and smile,' said Hippo. 'But some of us aren't the right shape for bowing, and smiling isn't enough by itself.'

'We could show the Princess how fast we can run,' said Giraffe.

'Or jump!' added Grasshopper. 'But some of us aren't very good at running *or* jumping.'

'We could cheer,' said Porcupine.

'Or trumpet!' added Elephant. 'But perhaps the Princess would be frightened.'

'We could dance,' said Secretary Bird.

Lion looked at Hippo and tried to imagine him dancing. He shook his head, and the animals stared at each other and sighed.

Small Brown Bird, who had listened quietly, opened his beak and chirruped shyly: 'Couldn't we make a garden, Lion? Princesses love flowers.'

Everyone stared at Small Brown Bird.

'That's quite a good idea,' said Lion. 'We can all help to make a garden.'

First, the animals chose a piccc of land.

'But it's much too rough,' said Lion. 'We must break up those big, hard lumps of earth.'

'I will do that,' cried Hippo at once. 'My feet are large and my body is heavy.' He stamped on the earth with his big feet, until it was smooth and fine.

'Good!' said Lion. 'Now we must make some tiny holes in which to plant the flower seeds.'

'I will do that,' Porcupine cried. 'The spines on my back are very sharp.' He curled himself into a prickly ball, and rolled over and over the earth until it was covered with tiny holes.

'Good!' said Lion. 'Now we must plant the seeds.'

'I will do that,' Grasshopper cried. 'I am light and quick.'

He jumped lightly and quickly over the earth, planting the seeds.

'Good!' said Lion. 'Now we must write the names of the flowers on wooden labels, so that we know which is which.'

'I will do that,' cried Secretary Bird. 'I have plenty of quills.'

He took one of the quills from his head, and wrote the names of the flowers on the labels.

'Good!' said Lion. 'Now we must water the garden all over.'

'I will do that,' Elephant cried. 'I will use my trunk.'

He filled his trunk at the river, and spouted water all over the garden.

'Good!' said Lion. 'Now we must keep a look-out for Monkey, so that he won't come and spoil our garden.'

'I will do that,' cried Giraffe. He stretched his long

neck, and peered this way and that, keeping a look-out for Monkey.

Small Brown Bird hung his head. He had wanted to help in making the garden. But it seemed that a small brown bird was useless for helping to make a garden.

The tiny seedlings began to grow. But when Lion

looked at the garden one day, he shook his head and growled in his throat.

'Those weeds that are growing are ugly,' he said. 'They will spoil our garden. Now who will pull out all those ugly weeds?'

None of the animals spoke at first. They looked at the ground and shuffled their feet. Then Hippo said in a sulky voice: 'I'm sure that *I* can't pull out the weeds. My feet are too big; they would crush the seedlings.'

'My spines would scratch the leaves,' said Porcupine.

'The weeds are much too heavy for me,' said Grasshopper.

'My stiff feather quills would bruise the buds,' said Secretary Bird.

'My trunk would break the stems,' said Elephant.

'It's no good looking at me,' said Giraffe. 'As you know very well, my neck is so long that I can't stoop down.'

The lazy animals turned their backs on the weeds.

Small Brown Bird flew down to the garden.

With his tiny beak he tugged at a weed, then flew away with the weed in his beak, and dropped it behind a prickly thorn bush. Then back he flew to the garden again to tug at another weed. All through the long, hot, tiring day, Small Brown Bird worked in the garden, pulling the weeds up one by one. The roots were strong and his beak was tiny, so the pile of weeds behind the thorn bush was still a very little one, when the sun went down behind the hills and

Small Brown Bird had to rest. But when he closed his eyes and slept, he dreamed that the Princess smiled at him kindly.

Day after day, Small Brown Bird weeded the garden. There were times when his wings ached with tiredness, and times when the weeds hurt his beak.

But one beautiful day, his work was finished. The pile of weeds behind the thorn bush was nearly as high as the thorn bush itself. Small Brown Bird looked at the garden, and not one weed could he see. The red and blue and yellow flowers had grown up straight and tall and lovely.

The very next day, Giraffe looked out over the trees and shouted: 'She's coming! I see her! The Princess is coming.'

The animals gathered around the garden, but Small Brown Bird flew to a tree, and peeped at the lovely Princess through the leaves.

The Princess smiled when she saw the garden.

'It's the prettiest garden I've ever seen. Did you really make it for me?' she said.

'Yes, we made it for you, Princess,' said the animals.

'The flowers are so straight and tall and lovely. You must have worked very hard indeed.'

'Yes, we worked very hard, Princess,' said the animals, smiling proudly.

'Will you give me some of your beautiful flowers? Now, who will pick them?' smiled the Princess.

Lion stepped forward.

'I told everyone what to do, so I should pick the flowers,' he said.

'I broke up the earth,' said Hippo.

'I made holes for the seeds,' said Porcupine.

'I planted the seeds,' said Grasshopper.

'I wrote the labels,' said Secretary Bird.

'I watered the garden,' said Elephant.

'I kept a look-out for Monkey,' said Giraffe.

The Princess smiled.

'Tell me,' she said. 'Who weeded the garden?'

None of the animals answered her question. They looked at the ground and shuffled their feet.

The Princess looked up at the tree in which Small Brown Bird was hiding. She saw two bright eyes and a tiny beak.

'Did you do the weeding, Small Brown Bird?' she asked with a smile.

Small Brown Bird nodded his head.

'Then you shall pick the flowers for me,' said the Princess.

Small Brown Bird flew down to the garden. With his tiny beak he picked a flower, and put it into the hands of the lovely Princess. He picked another and another until the Princess held a beautiful bunch of red and blue and yellow flowers.

Then the Princess kissed his small brown head, and smiled at him kindly. Small Brown Bird was very happy. He sang until the sun went down, and he never forgot the lovely Princess.

Stories of
Australian Animals

illustrated by Margery Gill

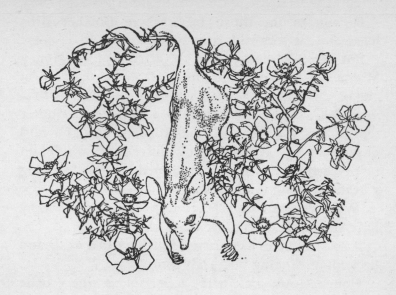

Honey Mouse

HONEY MOUSE sat by a tea-tree flower, and his tongue went flick, flick, flick, at the honey.

Then he curled the tip of his tail round a branch, and went swinging gently, upside down, to and fro, and to and fro.

Then there was nothing left to do.

'I shall go for a runabout,' he said. 'I shall see for myself what the birds are doing. Then I shall know why they sing and feel happy.'

He ran to the thorn bush where Butcher Bird lived, and sat very still, quietly watching.

Butcher Bird flew in the air, catching flies. Honey Mouse saw him come to the bush, to hook a fly on one of the thorns. Then back came the bird with a second fly, which he carefully hooked on another thorn. He caught and hooked, and caught and hooked, until seven flies hung on seven thorns. Then he perched on the bush and opened his beak, singing a beautiful song to himself.

'What were you doing?' Honey Mouse asked. 'Why have you hooked up those nasty black flies?'

'I collect them, of course,' Butcher Bird said, and he went on singing his lovely song.

Honey Mouse ran to the lonely place where little brown Bell Bird had his nest. Bell Bird hopped on his small brown toes, and his white throat throbbed as he sang to himself.

'You sing. So you're happy. Why?' asked Honey Mouse.

The stiff little tuft of perky black feathers on Bell Bird's head seemed to dance as he answered: 'Look at my nest. There it is. Just look.'

Honey Mouse looked at Bell Bird's nest. Crawling around it were six hairy caterpillars. Curl and stretch, curl and stretch, they slowly moved in soft fat loops.

'Oh!' said Honey Mouse. 'Do you like them?'

'Of course!' said Bell Bird. 'Of course! I collect them.'

Honey Mouse went to the heart of the forest, where Bower Bird lived in his neat little house.

Bower Bird's beak was full of wood ash. He used his yellow-tipped bill as a brush, painting black marks on the front of the house.

'I'm decorating my bower,' he said. 'It looks very beautiful, doesn't it, Honey Mouse?'

'Yes,' said Honey Mouse. 'Yes, it does. I suppose you will see to your garden next. It's full of untidy bits and pieces.'

Bower Bird stopped painting and looked at his garden. There on the ground, arranged in a pattern, were seven green snail shells, some bits of blue paper, four dead leaves, a parrot's blue feather, three green berries, and the handle of a tea-cup.

'Bit and pieces, indeed!' said Bower Bird. 'So *that's* what you call them, you poor little mouse. Those are my treasures. I searched the forest, day after day, in order to find them. They're beautiful things, and they're mine. I collect them.'

And Bower Bird sang a happy song.

Honey Mouse ran back home to his tea-tree.

'The birds are busy and happy,' he said. 'And now I know why. It's because they collect things.'

He wriggled his whiskers and smiled to himself.

'*I* shall collect things as well, and be happy.'

He twitched his nose. 'Not flies!' he said. 'Flies are far too black and nasty. Caterpillars are crawly and fat. Bits and pieces are *much* too untidy.'

But try as he would, he could think of nothing fit for a Honey Mouse to collect. So he went to the forest and sat on the ground, to the north of the tallest gum tree that grew. He tilted back his head, and called: 'Are you there? Will you tell me what *I* can collect?'

Out of the tree popped six fluffy heads, with small shining eyes and rubbery noses.

'Go away,' said the Koalas, and their heads popped into the tree again.

Honey Mouse sat to the south of the tree.

'But I can't think of *anything*. Please!' he said.

Six fluffy heads appeared.

'Go away!'

And six fluffy heads popped back in the tree.

Honey Mouse sat to the east of the tree.

'I'm only a little mouse,' he said. 'And I very much want to be happy. Please help me.'

Six pairs of eyes stared down from the tree. Then they disappeared, and a rustling began. Six little Koalas climbed up and up, snapping off gum tips to hold in their paws. Then they sat very still, and waited.

Honey Mouse sat to the west of the tree. 'I'll try to sing, then they'll listen,' he said. But he could not sing, so he squeaked instead:

> 'Nasty flies go buzz buzz buzz.
> Caterpillars crawl.
> What's the use of bits and pieces?
> No use at all.'

The Koalas lifted their paws, and they threw. They pelted Honey Mouse with gum tips.

'*Now* will you go away?' they said.

Honey Mouse covered his head with his paws, and the gum tips bounced and heaped around him. The only bits of Honey Mouse to be seen above the big green heap were his ears and eyes and twitching whiskers.

'Of course!' he said. 'Gum tips, of course! Thank you for helping me, Koalas. Gum tips are perfectly fit for a Honey Mouse. Yes. I like them. Of course! I'll collect them.'

Then Honey Mouse wanted to sing like a bird.

But he squeaked instead, and was just as happy.

Think, Mr Platypus

MR AND MRS PLATYPUS did not know where to make their home. They walked and talked and argued and searched, but they could not find anywhere fit for a platypus.

Mrs Platypus sighed, and said: 'Let's go and ask Blue-feathered Duck, because *she* has a beak and *we* have a beak.'

Blue-feathered Duck said: 'What an idea! How could you belong with us? We have feathers, and you have fur.'

'Come, my dear,' Mr Platypus said. 'We will go to the gum tree where Koala lives, because *he* wears fur and *we* wear fur.'

Koala was climbing the gum tree. Up-jump-up-jump-up-jump-up!

'Look! We have fur,' Mr Platypus called. 'Tell me, are gum trees pleasant to live in?'

Koala said: 'Look at your feet, Mr Platypus. Those are not feet for climbing a tree.'

Mr Platypus bent his head. He saw wide webbed feet, and beneath the soft skin there were claws, for digging into the earth.

'Yes,' he said. 'It is true, my dear. Our claws are the kind for digging down. Come, we must speak to little Echidna.'

Echidna was difficult to find. They could only see the tips of his prickles, for the rest of Echidna was under the ground.

'Excuse me!' Mr Platypus said. 'But could you come up for a minute, please? You will see we have digging feet, like yours.'

Up came Echidna, round and spiky, lifting his little snout in the air. Then he licked up ants with his pink ribbon tongue.

'How do *you* manage, I'd like to know, with that soft blunt beak of yours?' he asked. 'Why don't you go and eat worms, or something?'

'Worms!' Mr Platypus shook his head. 'Now who eats worms? Can you tell me, my dear?'

Mrs Platypus tried to be helpful.

'Kookaburra Bird eats snakes. They are little snakes, the same shape as worms.'

'Koo-ka-koo-ka-koo,' laughed Kookaburra. '*You* eat worms, and *I* eat snakes. But look at your funny fat furry legs. How could you perch on this thin branch, with those stumping, thumping, funny fat legs?'

'Really!' Mrs Platypus scolded. 'That young bird should learn some manners. I certainly don't intend to perch. We will talk to Wombat. *His* legs aren't skinny.'

'I see what you mean,' said Wombat politely. 'My legs are rather like yours, it is true. But I understand you lay eggs, Mrs Platypus. That makes a difference, don't you think? Perhaps you could talk to Snake. *She* lays eggs.'

Snake did not even try to explain. She simply hissed in an angry fashion: 'Stop being so silly and wasting my time. Sss!' And she glided away through the ferns.

'It's hopeless,' Mrs Platypus sighed. 'I really can't walk one more step.'

'Boo-book, boo-book!' said a voice from above. 'You are welcome to rest beneath my tree, but wouldn't you feel more comfortable in your own safe home, Mrs Platypus dear?'

'We have tried, Boobook Owl,' Mrs Platypus said. 'We have walked and talked and argued and searched, but we can't find a living place fit for a platypus.'

Owl poked her head, and her yellow eyes gleamed.

'Think, Mr Platypus, think,' she said. 'Stop this walking and talking and searching. Stop! And think, Mr Platypus, think. Where did your Father Platypus live? Where did your Grandfather Platypus live? Close your eyes and think, Mr Platypus.'

Mrs Platypus closed her eyes, and she fell asleep.

Mr Platypus closed his eyes, and started to think.

Very slowly, he seemed to remember. A picture

came into the back of his mind, a dark, cloudy picture that puzzled his brain. Very slowly, he saw it more clearly. And all at once it was perfectly plain.

'Ah!' he said. 'Ah yes! That's the place,' in such a contented, satisfied voice that Mrs Platypus opened her eyes.

'I have thought,' said Mr Platypus, 'and I have remembered. We are not ducks, to live on the river, or

koalas, to live in a tree. We are not echidnas, or kook-
aburras, or wombats, or hissing snakes, my dear. No!
We are just ourselves, of course. *You* are a platypus,
and *I* am a platypus. So where do we live? In a platypussary!'

Smiling large contented smiles, Mr and Mrs Platypus walked along beside the river to a place where it
widened into a pool.

'This is the place,' Mr Platypus said.

First they swam about in the pool, using their wide
webbed feet as paddles, and gobbling worms in their
big soft beaks. Then they felt strong, and ready to dig.
They tucked the soft webbing beneath their claws,
and started to dig a long, winding tunnel. The front
door opened under the water, and the back door
opened above the ground.

Scratch scratch scratch, Mr Platypus went.

'The floor is flat and the ceiling is curved. Yes, I
remember very well.'

Scratch scratch scratch, Mrs Platypus went.

'*I* have made a little round nursery.'

Off she went on her sturdy legs, collecting grasses
and rootlets and gum leaves, making a soft dry floor
for the nursery.

'There is one more thing to do,' she said.

She laid two eggs and curled around them, keeping
them warm with her soft, thick fur.

'Our babies will look like us,' she said. 'They'll be
safe, in this platypussary.'

'I will close the doors,' Mr Platypus said. And he
blocked them up with mud from the river.

Then Mr and Mrs Platypus looked at each other and smiled contentedly.

'Good-night, my dear,' Mr Platypus said.

'Good-night, my dear,' Mrs Platypus answered.

Then they went to sleep, in their platypussary.

Rabbits Go Riding

Up sprang Kangaroo, with long, strong leaps. And *down* came Kangaroo, thumping on the ground.

'Carry my leaves in your pocket,' called Koala, and he threw them into Kangaroo's pouch.

'They prickle,' said Kangaroo, but over the spinifex grass she leapt.

'Carry my ants,' called little Echidna, and he threw them into Kangaroo's pouch.

'They tickle,' said Kangaroo, but over the yellow wattles she leapt.

'Carry my frog in your pocket,' called Snake.

'It's cold and jumpy,' said Kangaroo, but on she went between the gum trees.

'Carry my pineapple,' Possum called.

'It's hard and lumpy,' said Kangaroo, but on she went, over scrubland and plain.

Kangaroo jumped with short, tired hops, with the leaves that prickled, the ants that tickled, the jumpy frog, and the lumpy pineapple. Her pouch looked just like a shopping basket.

'Now I am home at last,' she sighed, and she lay in the dust bath beneath her tree.

'Thank you,' the lazy creatures said. 'You can carry our things again tomorrow.'

'Oh, I'm so tired,' sighed Kangaroo. 'But they *will* keep throwing their things in my pouch.'

Then she lay in the shade and tried to sleep.

A little later she opened her eyes. Two fat rabbits sat side by side. Kangaroo saw that their fur was ruffled. Their paws were sore, and their tails were dusty.

'Please, Mrs Kangaroo,' they said. 'Which is the way to the farmer's grassland?'

Kangaroo looked towards the hills, which were blue, and misty, and far away.

'Between the gum trees and over the hills, at the end of a long black road,' she said.

The rabbits sat down on their dusty white tails, and stared at each other with tears in their eyes.

'Then we'll never get home tonight,' they said. 'We're tired, and lost, and a little bit frightened. We want to go home. We want it so much.'

Kangaroo looked at the sad little rabbits. Then she stretched her aching legs, and said: 'Jump in my pocket. I'll carry you home.'

The fat grey rabbits jumped in her pouch.

'We are ready to start, when you are,' they said.

Kangaroo jumped between the gum trees. The rabbits felt soft and warm in her pouch. They wriggled and giggled and squealed with delight.

'Thump, we are down, we are down,' they said. 'Up, we are up. We are down. We are up.'

'Carry my leaves in your pocket,' called Koala, and he threw them into Kangaroo's pouch.

'Rubbish,' giggled the fat grey rabbits, and they scooped up the leaves in their strong little paws, and threw them back at Koala.

Kangaroo reached the foot of the hills.

'Carry my ants,' called little Echidna, and he threw them into Kangaroo's pouch.

'Tickly things!' the rabbits squealed. 'They'll get in our fur.' And they threw them away.

Kangaroo leapt to the top of the hills.

'Carry my frog in your pocket,' called Snake, and he threw it into Kangaroo's pouch.

'Full up! No room!' called the fat grey rabbits, and they tossed the jumping frog in a salt bush.

Kangaroo reached the long black road.

'Carry my pineapple,' Possum called, and he threw it into Kangaroo's pouch.

'No thanks! We're not hungry,' the rabbits shouted, and the pineapple bounced as it fell on the road.

'Thump, we are down. We are up,' squeaked the rabbits. 'Thump, we are up. We are down. We are home.'

Kangaroo lay in the long cool grass. The rabbits climbed out of her pouch and said, 'We've had such a wonderful ride in your pocket. Thank you for bringing us home so quickly.'

Kangaroo smiled.

'It was easy,' she said. 'Those lazy creatures were *very* surprised. They won't make me carry their things again.'

She was right, and never, never again did her pouch look just like a shopping basket. Nor was it empty every day as she leapt over spinifex grass and hill, because over its edge peeped two furry faces.

'Here we go riding again,' squeaked the rabbits. 'Thump, we are down. We are up. We are down. Thump! We are riding in Kangaroo's pocket.'

Koala's Walkabout

KOALA sat in the crook of a tree under a roof of leaves, and he said:

'It's a pity to stay at home all day, when the sun is shining so brightly outside. So I think I'll go for a walkabout. I know I'm rather slow on my legs, but if I start early and don't waste time, I can get to the Blue Misty Mountains and back.'

Off went Koala between the trees, shuffling along on his slow furry legs. Some of his friends would have stopped to talk, but Koala said: 'No. I can't spare the time. I must hurry, hurry, all the way, or I shan't get back to my tree tonight.'

At the edge of the forest Koala saw Python Snake.

Python had tied himself into a knot. The more he tried to untangle himself, the tighter the knot became and the worse his temper got.

He wriggled and pulled in the wrong directions until it seemed he would burst with rage.

'Poor old Python is tangled,' said Koala. 'Who will help him? *I* can't stop.'

Koala walked on, but his steps were slow.

'How should *I* feel?' he said to himself. 'How should *I* feel, with a knot in my middle?'

And he turned around and hurried back to poor old struggling Python Snake.

'Do as I say,' he told the snake. 'Do as I say and I'll get you untangled.'

He looked at the knot from the left and the right.

Then he waved a paw in the air and said:

'That way! Wriggle a bit to the left. Yes, a bit more. That's it. That's the way.'

Then he waved his other paw, and said:

'Now, pull back. But very slowly. Back! And wriggle a bit to the right.'

Koala looked at the knot again.

'It's looser,' he said. 'You're getting untangled. Wriggle once more to the right, and you're straight.'

Python lay long and straight on the ground.

'I feel so comfortable,' he said. 'Thanks for the help.' And he glided away.

Koala's short legs went stumping along, trying to make up the time he had lost. But the Blue Misty

Mountains were far away when he came at last to the tangled scrubland. And then he saw Cassowary Bird, pushing and kicking his way through the scrub.

'Bother! Oh dear!' said the big black bird. 'Where did I put it? I really must find it.'

'What have you lost?' called Koala, as he stumped on his way across the scrub.

Cassowary called: 'An egg! Mrs Cassowary's egg! I promised to watch the egg, and I've lost it. At least, I haven't really lost it, but I just can't find it!'

And he got very angry and kicked at a bush.

'Cassowary is worried,' said Koala. 'But I really can't spare the time to help him. I must hurry, hurry, as fast as I can, if I want to get to the mountains and back.'

On he went, but his steps were slow.

'I don't lay eggs myself,' he said. 'But how should I feel if I did, and I lost one?'

He turned around and hurried back to worried Cassowary Bird.

'I think you should look very slowly and carefully,' he said. 'You look *that* way, and I'll look *this* way.'

Cassowary moved to the left, stepping gently, carefully searching. Koala moved to the right, very slowly, patting the grasses with careful paws.

'Look!' he shouted at last. 'What's this?'

He raised two paws above his head, and there between them, large and green, was Mrs Cassowary's egg.

'Put it down on the grass,' said the bird. 'Ah! It's a beautiful egg, don't you think? Thank you for finding it, Koala.'

The sun was already high in the sky as Koala hurried towards the rockland. The mountains were still a long way off, and Koala's paws were sore on the rocks. He was glad when he came to some tussocky grass.

'Now I can hurry, hurry,' he said.

Then he saw Bat. And Bat was frightened. His claw was caught in a tangle of grass, and he flapped and pulled as he tried to get free.

'I don't like the sun; it burns me,' he wailed. 'I want to go home to my cool dark cave, but I'm caught, and I'm burning. I think I shall die.'

Koala turned his face to the mountains.

'If I stop to help him my day will be spoiled. I'm very late already,' he said.

On he went, but his steps were slow.

'How should *I* feel?' he said to himself. 'How should *I* feel, caught in a tussock, burnt by the sun and a long way from home?'

And he turned around, and went back to Bat.

'Poor little Bat. Don't be frightened,' he said. 'I'll help you. You needn't be scared any more.'

He put his paws beneath Bat's wings, and gently pulled him away from the tussock.

'Thank you,' said Bat, as he fluttered away. 'Now I can go to my cave until night comes.'

Koala did not stop again, and at last he came to the Blue Misty Mountains. He rested, gazing with solemn eyes, warm and happy inside with gladness.

'So I *have* seen the Blue Misty Mountains,' he said.

Then he turned around, and set off for home.

87

He made his aching legs move fast, because dangerous things could happen at night to a little animal who was all by himself.

When he reached the edge of the rocky land, he knew he must rest, just for a minute. Most of the rocks were sharp and rough, so Koala was pleased when he saw a round shape that looked smooth and comfortable for sitting. He sighed as he rested his aching legs.

'I shall soon feel better again,' he said. 'This rock makes a very good seat for a koala.'

The rock rose up on four strong legs, and marched away, tipping and tilting, with Koala clinging to its back. It was *not* a rock, it was Great Green Turtle.

'Help!' cried Koala. 'Stop, Green Turtle. Let me get down. I shall fall on the rocks. I shall hurt myself dreadfully. Stop, Turtle, stop!'

But on went Turtle, tipping and tilting, while Koala clung to his slippery back.

Suddenly, out of the scrub glided Python, stretching his body in front of Turtle, long and straight, a great snake wall. And Turtle stopped. He could go no farther.

Koala clambered from Turtle's back, safe on his own four legs again.

'Thank you, Python Snake,' he said, and on he went across the scrub, with wobbly, aching, hurrying legs. There were strange dark shapes in the scrub at night.

Suddenly Koala shivered with fright. From behind

a bush came a strange new sound, a yelping, howling, horrible sound. And after the sound came two gleaming eyes. Wild Dog Dingo was on the prowl.

Koala turned around and ran. And after him, snapping sharp teeth, came Dingo.

Out of the scrub came Cassowary, kicking his legs and stretching his neck. He ran at howling Dingo Dog, and Dingo went yelping into the darkness.

Koala sat down for a very short rest.

'Thank you, Cassowary,' he said, and on he went, into the forest.

Koala's legs were dreadfully tired. He could hardly lift them off the ground.

'*That's* not my tree, I know,' he said. 'Neither is that, nor that, nor that. I shall *never* find my tree,' he said.

Out of the darkness came little black Bat, who liked to do his flying at night. *He* knew the trees in the moonlight.

He fluttered over Koala's head, then he glided away through the cool dark night. Koala followed, while black Bat swooped and fluttered ahead, leading the way through the strange dark forest.

Then all at once it was *not* a strange forest. It was Koala's forest, a friendly place. He saw his own strong sheltering tree, and he knew he was safe, and home again.

'Oh!' said Koala. 'Thank you, Bat.'

He climbed up into the crook of his tree, and curled himself into a sleepy bundle.

But before he closed his eyes he said:

'I know I'm rather slow on my legs, but I *did* see the mountains. I'm glad.'

Then he slept.

The Strange Tale of Quail

QUAIL BIRD could never make up his mind.

'Shall I or shan't I or shall I?' he said. 'Should I or would I or could I? Or won't I?'

But it did not help him. He could not decide.

One day Quail Bird said to himself: 'Today I'll be different. I'll make up my mind. I'll decide what to do, in my own clever head.'

He stood by a bush at the side of the road. Then he looked to the right and he looked to the left. And then he looked to the right again. He shuffled his feet on the ground and said:

'Shall I or shan't I?
Can I or can't I?
Shall I cross the road?'

He stood on his toes beside the bush, and made a short run, on the edge of the road.

Then he turned around, stood on his toes and made a short run, back to the bush.

Then he turned around, stood on his toes, and made a short run, away from the bush.

Then he turned around, stood on his toes, and Bang! Crash! Clatter! Hoot! The farmer's car rushed down the road. Quail was caught in a dusty whirlwind that sent him spinning into the air, whirling and twirling and squawking and squeaking, to the other side of the road.

Quail Bird shook the dust from his feathers. He looked around proudly and said to himself: 'Ah! You see. I'm a clever bird. I made up my mind. I *did* cross the road.'

Quail felt hungry. He wanted his dinner. He ran from one tuft of grass to the next, searching for seeds. He *always* ate seeds. Then Quail saw the seed, and he saw the red berry, side by side, on a bush. All his life he had eaten seeds; he had never fancied anything else. But now he looked at the berry and said:

'Should I or shouldn't I?
Could I or couldn't I?
Should I eat the berry?'

He stood on his toes, and made a small peck, at the berry.

Then he stood on his toes, and made a small peck, at the seed.

Then he stood on his toes, and made a small peck, at the berry.

Then he stood on his toes, and Swoop-swish-gulp! Top-knot Pigeon flew from the sky and gobbled up the ripe red berry.

Quail turned back to the seed and ate it.

'Ah!' he said. 'I'm a clever bird. I made up my mind. I should *not* eat the berry.'

Quail went looking for some one to talk to, and close to a rock he saw Snapping Turtle.

He kept his distance and said to himself:

'Would he or wouldn't he?
Could he or couldn't he?
Would he pull my tail?'

He stood on his toes, with his tail towards Turtle.

Then he stood on his toes, with his beak towards Turtle.

Then he stood on his toes, with his tail towards Turtle.

Then he stood on his toes, and Snap-tug-crack! Turtle had pulled out his very best feather.

Quail ran away and hid in a grass tussock.

'Ah!' he said. 'I'm a clever bird. I made up my mind. He *would* pull my tail.'

Quail felt tired. It was long past his bedtime.
He stood by the tussock of grass and said:

> 'Will I or won't I?
> Do I or don't I?
> *Will* I go to sleep?'

He stood on his toes, and closed his eyes.
Then he stood on his toes, and opened his eyes.
Then he stood on his toes, and fell asleep.
Quail was quite a clever bird. He had made up his
mind. He *did* go to sleep.

Brolga Bird Dances

BROLGA BIRD danced by the witchetty bush.

He kicked his legs forwards and sideways and backwards, bobbing and hopping and twisting and skipping, all by himself, by the witchetty bush.

'Now I shall rest until sunset,' he said.

Over the plain scuttled little grey Mole, sniffing the air and looking for insects.

'Brolga, will you dance?' he asked.

'I'll dance at sunset,' Brolga told him.

Under the fern trees came fat brown Wombat, shuffling along on his hairy legs.

'Brolga, when will you dance?' he asked.

'I'll dance when the sun goes down,' said Brolga.

Between the spinifex grasses ran Gecko, kicking the sand with his frisky feet.

'Dance for me, Brolga Bird,' he called.

'Not until sunset,' Brolga told him.

Across the scrub came furry Possum, his gentle brown eyes on the look-out for danger.

'Dance for me Brolga, please,' he called.

'I have said it before. I will say it again. I will dance when the sun goes down,' said Brolga. 'Come back to watch me. And don't forget.'

Mole and Wombat and Gecko and Possum said: 'No, of course we shan't forget.'

'I think that you *will* forget,' said Brolga. '*I* am the only one that remembers. Come over here. I'll tie string on your tails.

> 'String on your tails! So you won't forget.
> Brolga will dance when the sun has set.'

Mole and Wombat and Gecko and Possum turned their tails towards Brolga Bird. On each of the tails he tied pieces of string, fixing them tightly with neat little bows.

'Good-bye,' he called. 'I shall dance at sunset. Don't be afraid that I shan't remember. I am the one that *always* remembers.'

After the string had been tied to his tail, little grey Mole scuttled far away, his tiny stiff tail pointing up at the sun. He came to a place where the mulga grass grew, and there he sat on a sandy patch, being very careful to keep quite still.

'My tail is so short and the string is so long. It could easily slip right off,' he said.

The sun rose high in the hot blue sky, and Mole began to prickle all over.

Up he jumped, and his tiny front legs scooped out a hole in the soft yellow sand. Very soon he was out of the sun, with the sand lying smooth and cool on his back. He wriggled, and smiled, and fell asleep.

When he opened his eyes, the sun was setting.

'It is time to go and watch Brolga,' he said.

Off he went, with his tail pointed upwards, marching along and happily singing:

'String on my tail! So I shan't forget.
Brolga will dance when the sun has set
Brolga is clever.
Brolga will never
Never, ever forget.'

Then Mole turned around, and the string was not there.

In a flash he was back where the mulga grass grew, scratching and scooping and flinging the sand up.

'But I'll never find that string,' he said. 'Brolga would scold me. I'll stay where I am.'

So Mole did not go to the witchetty bush.

After the string had been tied to his tail, fat brown

Wombat shuffled away to his burrow beside an old grey tree stump.

'Good! It is getting hot,' he said, and he stretched himself out on the ground to sunbathe.

He closed his eyes as the sun rose high, but after an hour or so he grunted.

'Bother that string. It hurts,' he said.

Wombat's tail was short and stumpy, so Brolga had tied on the string extra tightly, in order to keep it from slipping off.

'It pinches,' said Wombat. 'It hurts my poor tail. I'll take it right off, and tie it on loosely.'

He turned around to reach the string, but as he turned, his tail turned too. He growled, and snatched, and off came the string.

'That feels a great deal better,' sighed Wombat. 'Now I can tie the string loosely – I think.'

He turned around to reach his tail, but his tail turned too, and he could not catch it. He turned

around faster, and so did his tail. It was always behind him. He growled, and stamped.

'Bother!' he said, and tossed the string upwards
into a gum tree.

Then he lay down. He was hot and tired.

'Brolga will scold me.
"Keep it," he told me.
"Then you will come." '

Wombat winked one shining eye.

'But I *won't* come,' he said. 'I am much too tired.'

And he closed his eyes and fell asleep, and he did
not go to the witchetty bush.

After the string had been tied to his tail, Gecko ran
away to the bushland. He sat on a rock pretending to
sleep, but his little black eyes were waiting and watching. A gnat hummed lazily by in the sunshine, and
flick! it was gone, and Gecko was smiling.

'Squawk!' said White Cockatoo from a tree.
'Squawk! It's dinner-time. *I'm* hungry too. Give me
that worm, because *you* don't want it.'

'I haven't got it.' Gecko said. 'Where is a worm?'
And he stared around him.

'There! On your tail,' said White Cockatoo.

'Nonsense,' said Gecko. 'That's string, not a worm.'

'Squawk squawk squawk,' scolded White Cockatoo.
'It's a worm. It wriggled. I say it's a worm.'

She swooped from the tree, and Gecko ran. Then
Gecko suddenly jerked in the air, and landed on an
old grey tree stump. He sat so still that he hardly
breathed.

'Now I am part of the tree stump,' he said. 'And my tail is a leaf. It *looks* like a leaf.'

Cockatoo stopped. At first she seemed puzzled. Then she said: 'Ah! There's a leaf on that stump. Ah! There's a nice wriggly worm on that leaf.'

Jab went her curving beak at the string.

'Oh!' squealed Gecko. 'You're jabbing my tail.'

But Cockatoo planted her toes on the ground, and pulled at the string with all her strength.

'Oh!' squealed Gecko. 'Stop it, I tell you.'

Suddenly White Cockatoo fell backwards.

'I've got it, I've got it, I've got it!' she squawked.

Gecko looked up. Cockatoo flew above him. Dangling down from her beak was the string, and tied to the string was Gecko's tail.

Gecko sighed as he lay in the sunshine.

'That's the end of that,' he said. 'And that's the end of my tail, as well.

> 'Cockatoo has got the string,
> The string has got my tail.
> So – it's going to be a bother,
> But I'll have to grow another.'

Gecko lay in the sunshine, and slept, waiting for his tail to grow. So *he* did not go to the witchetty bush.

After the string had been tied to his tail, Possum darted home to his tree. Mrs Possum was feeding the seven babies, so Possum hung by his tail from a branch.

Mrs Possum finished her work.

'What is that thing on your tail?' she asked.

'Yes. What is that thing?' squealed the seven babies.

'It's a string, not a thing,' Possum said, swinging gently to and fro. 'Brolga has asked me to watch while he dances, and he gave me this string. So that I shan't forget.'

When bedtime came, the babies were naughty.

'We're not a bit sleepy. We want to play.'

'We want that string to play with,' they shouted.

'It's a very important string,' said Possum. 'You must play with a leaf.'

'No,' wailed the babies. 'We want that string.'

'Let them have it,' begged Mrs Possum. 'You can take it back when they've gone to sleep.'

Possum slowly untied the string. The babies snatched it, squealing with joy. They tugged it and chewed it and scratched it and clawed it, and broke it into seven pieces.

Then they slept.

Possum could only sigh, and murmur:

'String is broken, and I know
Brolga Bird would scold me. So
I shall just forget to go.'

So *none* of them went to the witchetty bush.

Brolga stood by the bush, and waited.

As soon as the sun began to set, he held out his silver-grey feathered wings.

'Now I am ready to dance,' he said. 'I haven't forgotten. I *always* remember. And those creatures will come very soon, I expect. They have string on their tails, so they won't forget, Brolga will dance when the sun has set.'

But Mole and Wombat and Gecko and Possum did not come to the witchetty bush.

Brolga fluttered his silver wings. He kicked his legs forwards and sideways and backwards, bobbing and

hopping and twisting and skipping, all by himself, by the witchetty bush.

Then, because they happened to be passing, Mouse and Rabbit and Parrot and Turtle stopped by the witchetty bush to watch him.

'Ah!' said Brolga. 'I see you have come after all.'

And Brolga Bird, who never forgot, danced beside the witchetty bush.

Kangaroo Joey Finds his Shadow

'I SHAN'T get up,' said Kangaroo Joey.

'Yes, you must,' his mother scolded. 'Up! At once! Do you hear? Get up.'

Joey climbed from his mother's pouch.

'It's cold and nasty out here,' he grumbled. 'I'm only a *little* Kangaroo.'

'Don't be a baby,' smiled Kangaroo Mother. 'You're a big Joey now. You weigh down my pocket. You must learn to hop on your own strong legs, because *I* can't carry you all the time.'

Kangaroo Mother leapt in the air. Then down she came to the ground. Thump!

'You see?' she said. 'Like that! It's easy.'

'Uh!' said Joey. 'Huh!' And he jumped.

But he fell on his ears in a clump of grass.

'No, I don't like it,' he said. 'I shan't do it.'

Kangaroo Mother did not spank him. She had spanked him before, and it did no good. So she and Joey ate grass for breakfast, while the sun came up and warmed their backs.

Then Kangaroo Mother said: 'Climb in my pocket. I'll carry you to smoother grass. Then you can practise your jumps again.'

Joey smiled as he climbed in her pouch, because he meant to stay there, for ever.

Kangaroo Mother leapt and thudded, and Joey decided to go to sleep.

But all at once he saw the shadow.

'Look!' he shouted, pointing a paw. And he nearly fell out of his mother's pocket.

When Kangaroo Mother leapt in the air, the shadow slid on the ground below them, and when she thudded down to the ground, the shadow lay still, quietly waiting.

'Slide and stop,' sang Kangaroo Joey. 'Slide and stop. It's following us.'

By the time they reached the smoother grass, Kangaroo Joey was wriggling with laughter.

'That shadow has followed us, slide and stop, slide and stop. I think it likes us.'

'I am sure it likes *me*,' said Kangaroo Mother. 'It's my very own shadow. That's why it follows me.'

'Oh!' said Joey. 'I wish it were mine. Can't I borrow it, just for today?'

Kangaroo Mother smiled, and said: 'No. It is much too big for you, Joey. You must find your own shadow, to fit your own size. It is waiting for you, there on the grass.'

'*I* can't see it,' said Kangaroo Joey, screwing up his eyes. 'Where is it?'

'Get out and look,' said Kangaroo Mother.

Joey tumbled out of her pouch, and sat on the patch of sunlit grass. And there behind him, quietly waiting, was a small black shadow, all his own.

'I like it,' said Joey. 'And I think it likes me.'

He hopped, and his shadow slid beneath him. Down he came, plop! And his shadow lay still.

'Good! I've got you, shadow,' said Joey. 'You can't get away. I'm sitting on you. Now, come along, shadow. I'm going to hop. Come along, follow me. Come along, shadow.'

Kangaroo Joey hopped and plopped, and the shadow slid along and stopped.

When Joey ate his dinner, and rested, the shadow lay on the ground beside him.

Then Kangaroo Joey hopped again. Hop and plop. Slide and stop. All day long he and his shadow moved across the sunlit grass.

Kangaroo Mother called: 'Time to go home! You and your shadow must go to sleep.'

Then Kangaroo Mother and Kangaroo Joey set off side by side towards home, with their very own shadows, one big, one small.

The Bird that Wore Stripes

THE chick that wore black and white stripes on his back walked through the grass, and said to himself:

'I must find my name, a big, grand name, because when I grow up I shall be a big bird.'

He went to the Blue-tongued Lizard, and said:

'Please can you help me to find my name?'

'Open your beak,' said the Blue-tongued Lizard. 'No. Your tongue isn't blue, like mine. So your name isn't Blue-tongued Bird, that's certain. But the feathers grow striped black and white on your back. Perhaps your name is Stripey-feathers.'

'Yes,' said the chick. 'Yes. It might be that. Stripey-feathers!' And off he went.

He stood on the bank of a green lagoon, watching long-legged Spoonbill Bird wading among the reeds in the water.

'Hello!' he called. 'I'm Stripey-feathers. That's my name. I like it. Do you?'

The big bird looked at the little bird.

'Well, you certainly aren't a Spoonbill,' he said. 'Your beak doesn't look like a spoon. It's stubby. How would Stubby-beak do for a name?'

'Yes,' said the chick. 'I like that, too. I'll be Stripey-feathers Stubby-beak.'

Off he went to the edge of the stream, and there he saw Willy Wagtail Bird.

'Hello, Wagtail,' he said. 'Do you know me? I am Stripey-feathers Stubby-beak.'

Wagtail flicked his tail, and said: 'I can see your stripes and your stubby beak, but where is your tail? You've forgotten to wear it. Tail-forgotten should be your name.'

'Oh!' said the chick. 'Perhaps it should. So I'm Stripey-feathers Stubby-beak Tail-forgotten. That's my name.' And he smiled to himself and went to the grassland.

Carpet Snake came sliding along, but he stopped when he saw the stripey bird.

'Who are you? You're new,' he said.

'Yes,' said the bird. 'But I've found my name. It's Stripey-feathers Stubby-beak Tail-forgotten. Do you like it?'

'Not very much,' said Carpet Snake. 'But I see that you certainly can't be a Carpet Bird. You trot on your legs instead of sliding. Why don't you call yourself Trotty-legs?'

'Oh, what a very good name,' said the chick. 'I'll be Stripey-feathers Stubby-beak Tail-forgotten Trotty-legs.'

And off he went to the wattle trees.

'Hello, Fairy Wren,' he said.

The little blue bird that danced in the air fluttered down to a branch, and said:

'I haven't seen you here before. What is your name? Have you found it, big chick?'

'Yes,' said the chick. 'And it's big, like me. It's Stripey-feathers Stubby-beak Tail-forgotten Trotty-legs.'

He waited for Fairy Wren to say 'Good.'

But Fairy Wren did not say 'Good.' She said: 'Bad! It is bad for a fairy to be so big. So you can't be a dancing Fairy Bird. You are not a fairy, are you, chick?'

'No,' said the chick. 'I am Not-a-fairy. So I'm Stripey-feathers Stubby-beak Tail-forgotten Trotty-legs Not-a-fairy. Is that better?'

But the little blue bird was dancing again, and the chick turned away and went to a tea-tree, where Honey Mouse was eating his dinner.

'Hello,' said the chick.

'Hello,' said Honey Mouse. '*You* don't eat honey, do you, Bird?'

'I've never tried it,' the stripey chick said. 'I usually eat red berries for dinner, and my name isn't Bird. It's better than that. It's Stripey-feathers Stubby-beak Tail-forgotten Trotty-legs Not-a-fairy. That's my name.'

'I don't think it's right,' said Honey Mouse. 'I'm a mouse that eats honey. I'm Honey Mouse. You're a bird that eats berries. You're Berry-bird.'

'Why, so I am,' said the stripey chick. 'I'm Stripey-feathers Stubby-beak Tail-forgotten Trotty-legs Not-a-fairy Berry-bird. And I think that's enough, for ever and ever.'

Off went the chick to the forest trees, and he felt very proud of his big new name.

'I shall tell it to everyone I meet. They will like to hear it,' he said to himself.

He met Wombat and Cuscus, but neither of them could say his name, because it was too long to remember.

The chick stood all alone in the forest, and he felt very sad as he said to himself: 'My big new name is just a nuisance. It's much too long for my friends to say. So now I must start all over again, to find a name that is short and easy.'

He sighed, and said: 'I'm tired of searching. I shall ask the very next creature I see, and whatever they say, that is my name.'

Between the trees ran little Brown Rat.

'Rat,' called the chick. 'Tell me my name.'

But Rat took no notice. He ran for his life, squeaking: 'Ee ee ee. I must run. Ee ee.'

Behind him ran Wild Cat, his long tail waving.

'Cat,' called the chick. 'I haven't a name.'

Cat did not care. He ran after Rat, calling: 'Mew. I must catch him. Mew mew mew.'

'Oh dear,' said the chick. 'They won't even answer. I don't think I'll *ever* find a name.'

'Ee,' said Rat, as he raced through the trees.

'Mew,' said Cat, as he chased close behind.

The chick stretched up on his strong little legs, his beak lifted proudly, his neck very straight. At last he had found his very own name.

'Ee,' said Rat.

'Mew,' said Cat, far away in the heart of the forest.

'Ee,' said the chick.

'Mew,' said the chick.

'Ee and mew. That's what they said. So Emu's my name. Emu! I like it.'

He kept this new name and liked it, for ever and ever.

The Laughing Bird

WHEN Kookaburra was only a chick, his mother said:

'You must learn to laugh.'

'Koo-ka-koo,' said Kookaburra.

'Louder, and longer!' his mother said. "Koo-ka-koo-ka-koo. Like that.'

Kookaburra tried again, and a sad little croak came out of his beak. But he practised and practised all day long, until at last he could laugh very well.

'Koo-ka-koo-ka-koo,' he gurgled. 'I laugh when I'm happy, and I laugh when I'm sad.'

He flew away between the gum trees.

'Koo-ka-koo-ka-koo,' he chuckled. 'Listen, I'm the laughing bird.'

With a swish and swoop of small green wings, some budgerigars came chattering down, to drink and splash in a waterhole.

Kookaburra smiled to himself.

'Koo-ka-koo-ka-koo,' he said. 'Hello, Budgies. Aren't I clever?'

The budgies lifted their blunt little beaks. Up they swooped at Kookaburra, slapping their spiky green wings in his face, and chirping angrily: 'Go away. Don't laugh at *us*, you impertinent bird.'

Kookaburra flew away. 'I'm really a laughing bird,' he said. 'What does impertinent mean, I wonder?'

He flew to the forest where Brush Turkey lived. Fat green Turkey was ruffled and busy. Her tail was turned to a pile of leaves, and her feet kicked and jerked and scraped at the ground, busily flinging more leaves on the heap.

Kookaburra sat on a branch.

'I think you are making a mountain,' he said.

'Mustn't stop, mustn't stop. Busy!' said Turkey. 'I've just laid some eggs. I must cover them up. Eggs must keep warm. I must cover them up.'

Kookaburra watched and wondered.

'So that's how you hatch your eggs,' he said. 'It's clever. I can be clever, too. Listen, green Turkey. Stop working, and listen.'

Kookaburra opened his beak.

'Koo-ka-koo-ka-koo,' he chuckled.

Brush Turkey's feathers bristled with anger. She

kicked her big feet in the forest floor, flinging up leaves at Kookaburra.

'How dare you laugh at *me*?' she scolded. 'Of course I hatch my eggs like this. It isn't funny, impertinent bird.'

Kookaburra flew away.

'I don't know why she scolded,' he said. 'I don't even know what impertinent means.'

He went to the swamp, where the blue lilies grew. Suddenly they rocked on the water, and Jabiru Stork came striding along, slanting his long black beak like a sword.

Jab! And a fish was a bulge in his throat.

'Got it! Well caught!' called Kookaburra. '*I'm* going to learn to fish like that, now that we've finished the laughing lessons. Koo-ka-koo-ka-koo. Do you like it? That's what I learnt, and I tried very hard.'

Jabiru ruffled his black and white feathers. Then he stretched out his wings and splashed through the water, slanting his beak at Kookaburra.

'Be off, or I'll jab you,' he scolded. 'I'll jab you. Be off or be jabbed, you impertinent bird.'

'I only laughed,' said Kookaburra. 'I don't understand.' And he flew away.

Deep in the forest Lyre Bird danced, and Kookaburra stopped to watch. Lyre Bird danced on a leafy hill, backwards and forwards, step and stop. Then slowly he spread out his feathery tail, out and out above his body, until it looked like a white umbrella. And as he danced, his tail danced too, in a white, shimmering, beautiful mist.

'Oh!' sighed Kookaburra. 'Oh! Koo-ka-koo.'

He could say no more.

Lyre Bird closed his beautiful tail. And he opened his beak, making strange, ugly sounds.

'Ah! That's the axe. Listen! Your tree is being chopped. They're chopping it down with an axe. Do you hear? You'd better go home and search for your mother, instead of laughing, impertinent bird.'

Kookaburra flew very fast.

'What have they done to my tree?' he said. 'Where is my mother? I hope I can find her.'

But his mother was safe on the home tree, smiling.

'Oh!' sighed Kookaburra. 'Oh!'

And he flew down and perched on the branch beside her.

'I hope you remembered to laugh,' she said.

'Yes, I remembered,' said Kookaburra. 'But nobody seemed to like my voice. They said I was just an impertinent bird. What does it mean, an impertinent bird?'

'Forget about it,' his mother said. 'But never forget to laugh.'

Next day the sun shone bright and hot, but Kookaburra did not laugh. Day after day the sun burned the grass, and when the budgies flew down with limp wings, they found their waterhole dried into mud.

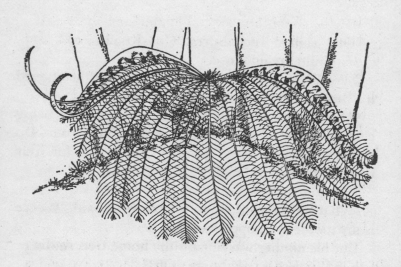

They crouched on the ground with open beaks, and green wings dragging in the dust.

Brush Turkey stopped her kicking and scraping. She panted for breath in the shade of a bush, forgetting about her precious eggs.

Jabiru stood quite still in the swamp. The lily petals turned grey, and beneath them, the fish lay dying in the mud.

Lyre Bird's white feathers were draggled and dusty. He thought that never again would he dance, and never again would the cool rain fall.

Day after day the hot sun burned. The birds did not sing. They crouched on the ground, searching the bright blue sky for clouds. The grass was burned brown and the flowers died away.

Kookaburra sat by his mother, thirsty in the blazing sun.

'Laugh,' said his mother. 'Laugh, Kookaburra.'

'I can't,' he said. 'My throat is dry. I'm hot, and afraid, and very unhappy.'

'When you were happy, you laughed,' said his mother. 'Now you are sad. But still you must laugh.'

Kookaburra opened his beak.

'Koo-ka-koo-ka-koo,' he said. 'Koo-ka-koo.' And his dry throat ached.

The budgies lifted their dusty heads.

Brush Turkey left the shade of the bush.

Jabiru strode through the muddy swamp.

Lyre Bird spread out his tail, and danced.

'Kookaburra laughs,' they said. 'He certainly can't be laughing at *us*. And he can't feel happy. No one is happy. So Kookaburra's the only one who is brave enough to laugh when he's sad.'

Across the sky came a small grey cloud. Then another came, and yet another. Down to the earth splashed the silver raindrops, filling the swamp and the waterhole, cooling the earth and the birds' dusty feathers.

The budgies splashed and drank in the waterhole, Brush Turkey happily scratched and kicked, Jabiru swallowed his supper of fish, and Lyre Bird danced in the heart of the forest.

'And Kookaburra laughs,' they said. 'He laughs when he's happy and he laughs when he's sad. We hope he will *always* laugh. We like it.'

Lizard Comes Down from the North

'Happy days!' said little green Lizard, flicking his tiny tail in the air. 'I'm going to the forest. Oh, happy days!'

And he pattered along on his stumpy legs.

'It's a long, long journey I'm making,' he said. 'Over bushland and sand and grassland and scrub.'

And he hopped in the air with a squeak of delight, because he felt gay and brave and adventurous.

Then Lizard looked up against the sun, and far above him the black-feathered swan beat his wings in the air, and called: 'Why are you coming down from the north, you strange little thing with a scaly back?'

But Lizard heard only the beat of strong wings as Swan flew away. So on he pattered.

Black Swan came to the sandy desert.

'I mustn't fly over the sand,' he said, and he called to Kangaroo Mouse below: 'Mouse-with-a-pocket, take my message. Go to the forest and tell them there that a creature is coming down from the north. He has scales on his back, and a flicking tail, and he's walking along on his sturdy legs.'

Mouse jumped away towards the forest. Faster and faster and faster she raced, until at last her spindle-thin legs were springing so fast that they could not be seen, and she seemed to be a ball of fur, twirling and whirling and blown by the wind.

Then Kangaroo Mouse reached tussocky grassland, and she stopped. She sat by a tuft of grass and said: 'It's twice as tall as myself *and* my tail, and it's thick and prickly. I can't go on. These kind of jumps are for *real* kangaroos.'

'Did you call me?' asked Kangaroo.

'No,' said Mouse. 'But I'm glad you're here. Go to the forest and take my message. A creature is coming down from the north. He has big shining scales and a beating tail, and he's walking along on his big strong legs.'

Kangaroo leapt towards the forest, crushing the grass beneath his feet. He came to the scrubland, and there he stopped. He saw spiky thickets, and thorny stems.

'Cassowary!' Kangaroo called. And out of the scrub came the great black bird. 'Cassowary, take my message. A creature is coming down from the north. He has great shining scales, and a huge beating tail, and he's marching along on his mighty legs.'

Cassowary turned to the scrub. He was not afraid
of its spikes and thorns.

'I'm a fighting, biting, battling bird. I can push
through worse than this,' he said.

He pushed and kicked through the spiky scrub,

until he saw the forest ahead. He ran through the trees, and before very long he saw Bower Bird, Possum, Platypus, Turkey, and Wombat.

'Listen,' he said. 'Here is my message. A creature is coming down from the north. He has huge shining scales, and a great lashing tail, and he's crashing along on enormous legs.'

The creatures stared at each other, and trembled.

'It's a dragon,' said Bower Bird.

'He'll eat us,' said Possum.

'Help!' said Platypus.

'Save us,' said Turkey.

'What a hullaballoo,' said Wombat.

Cassowary stamped his foot.

'You make me angry, you foolish creatures. Talking will do no good,' he said. 'Why don't you stir yourselves up, and *do* something?'

And he stamped away angrily back to the scrub.

'We must frighten the dragon away,' said Bower Bird.

"We must make a scarecrow to scare him,' said Possum.

'We don't want to scare a *crow*,' said Platypus.

'Then we'll make a scaredragon,' Turkey said.

'What a to-do and a fuss,' said Wombat.

They stuck the branch of a tree in the ground, for the scaredragon's body. Then they stuck a pineapple on to the branch, for the scaredragon's head.

But still they felt frightened.

'We must hide behind a wall,' said Bower Bird.

'And look out over the top,' said Possum.

'And when we hear the dragon coming, we'll shout, and wave our paws,' said Platypus.

'And make our faces look fierce,' said Turkey.

'What a hurry and scurry,' said Wombat.

The creatures began to make a wall.

They stuck a row of sticks in the ground, and Bower Bird, who knew about such things, fixed creepers and stems and twigs between them.

Possum banged the wall with his paw, to see if it was strong and safe.

Platypus filled the cracks with mud.

Turkey scraped up a pile of leaves, building them up behind the wall.

Wombat ran around in circles.

'Now we *ought* to be safe,' they said.

They stood in a row on the pile of leaves, looking out over the top of the wall.

And they waited, and waited, and waited.

Into the forest came little green Lizard, flicking his tiny tail in the air.

'Happy days!' he smiled to himself. 'I've come to the forest. Oh, happy days!' And he pattered along on his stumpy legs.

'It's a long, long journey I've made,' he said. 'Over bushland and sand and grassland and scrub.'

He hopped in the air with a squeak of delight, because he felt happy and safe and friendly.

Then Lizard looked up.

And he saw the scaredragon.

'What is that pineapple doing?' he said. 'Just sitting quite still, all alone, on a stick?'

He saw the wall, and over the top of it, the faces of
Bower Bird, Possum, Platypus, Turkey, and Wombat.

'And what are *you* doing, up there?' he asked.

The five faces stared back at little green Lizard.

'We're hiding away from the dragon,' said Bower
Bird.

'He's coming down from the north,' said Possum.

'He'll eat us all up if he can,' said Platypus.

'He has huge shining scales, and a great lashing
tail, and he's crashing along to the forest,' said Turkey.

'*What* a time we've had!' said Wombat.

Lizard's small scales shone green in the sun as he

flicked his tiny tail in the air. Then he pattered behind the wall, and said:

'Please may I hide behind your wall? I'm not very fond of dragons, myself.'

So Bower Bird, Possum, Platypus, Turkey, Wombat, and Lizard looked out over the top of the wall, waiting for the dragon to come.

And they waited, and waited, and waited.

Far away, a dead branch fell, crashing down to the forest floor.

'The dragon! It's coming,' the creatures cried.

They shouted, and flapped their paws about, and made fierce faces, until they were tired.

Then they all said: 'Sh!' and 'Listen!' and 'Hush!'

They kept very still behind the wall, and the only sound they heard was a plop! as a ripe red berry fell to the ground.

'Hurrah!' cried Bower Bird. 'We've done it! We've done it! We've scared the dreadful dragon away.'

'He's crashing back to the north,' said Possum.

'He'll never come *here* again,' said Platypus.

'We're really rather clever,' said Turkey.

'Clever and brave and fierce!' said Wombat.

Lizard did not say a word. He had disappeared behind a tree.

He looked at his little shining scales, and his flicking tail, and his stumpy legs.

He looked, and he thought very hard.

And he guessed.

'Oh my, I'm a dragon, I am!' he said. 'Oh ho! I'm a dragon. A great fierce dragon!'

Then Lizard flicked his tiny tail, and he rolled on the ground with his legs in the air, laughing and laughing and laughing.

Stories of
South American Animals

illustrated by Charlotte Hough

The Little Yellow Jungle Frogs

THE four little yellow frogs sang to each other.

'Her-grok-grak. What a beautiful day!'

Then the four little frogs danced on the river bank. Hop-step-kick in the warm yellow sand.

Mrs Turtle came from the river, and scooped out a hole in the sandy bank. Then she laid some eggs in the hole, and said: 'Good! Now I must hide them to keep them safe.'

She shuffled her feet, pushing sand in the hole until she was sure that the eggs were covered. Taking great care, she patted the sand until it was flat and smooth again.

'Now I am tired. I shall sleep,' she said.

'Her-grok-grak,' sang the yellow frogs. 'Her-grok-grak. What a beautiful day!'

'Oh, do be quiet,' sighed Mrs Turtle. 'Don't you see that I'm trying to sleep?'

'Then we'll dance, instead,' said the yellow frogs. 'We'll dance on that smooth little patch of sand.'

Hop-step-kick danced their yellow feet. Hop-step-kick. And up flew the sand.

Mrs Turtle opened her eyes.

'Stop it! Stop it at once!' she scolded. 'I took great care to smooth the sand, so that no one would see that my eggs were there. You naughty frogs have spoiled my work, and now I must do it all over again.'

The four little frogs looked down at their feet.

'Let's go back to the jungle,' they said. 'Then we'll sing and dance as much as we like, without disturbing Mrs Turtle.'

They sat in the jungle beneath a tree.

'Her-grok-grak,' they sang to each other. 'Her-grok-grak. We sing very loudly.'

But up in the tree sat Howler Monkey.

'Oh do be quiet, you little frogs, with your very little voices,' he said.

Then Howler Monkey began to howl, and the sound that he made was as loud as the wind when it tore at the tops of the jungle trees.

'Oh!' squeaked the little yellow frogs. 'Your voice is certainly louder than ours. But see how we dance. And *you* can't dance.'

Hop-step-kick danced the little frogs. Hop-step-kick around the tree.

'Oh, do stop dancing around my tree. You are making me feel quite giddy,' said Monkey. 'And if I get

giddy and fall on your heads, I shall squash you flat. So stop it! At once!'

The four little frogs sat still, and sighed.

'Let's go away to the lake,' they said. 'Then we'll sing and dance as much as we like, without annoying Howler Monkey.'

At the edge of the lake sat big brown Toad, staring down at the still, clear water.

'Her-grok-grak,' sang the yellow frogs. 'Her-grok-grak. The sun is shining.'

'Please! Do stop that noise,' said Toad. 'I was looking into the lake mirror. I thought and thought, and just for a minute I thought that my face was beautiful. Then along you came, making a noise, and I couldn't think any more. You spoilt it.'

Two big tears shone in Toad's eyes, and fell plip, plop, in the lake.

The four little yellow frogs stared at Toad.

'Oh dear! We're truly sorry,' they said. 'Watch us dance on these little grey pebbles.'

Hop-step-kick danced the yellow frogs. Hop-step-kick. And up flew the pebbles.

Plip, plip, plop, they fell in the water, breaking the lake into shining ripples.

'Oh, stop it, stop it, stop it,' wailed Toad. 'Now you are spoiling the lake mirror.'

The four little frogs were truly sorry.

'Let's go away to the stream,' they said. 'Then we'll sing and dance as much as we like, without upsetting poor old Toad.'

The four little frogs went to the stream.

Three green parrots sat on a bush, and Humming Bird was talking to them.

'Look at my wings. I move them quickly, so that they hum,' she told the parrots.

'Squawk,' said the parrots. 'Yes, we hear.'

'No other bird in the world can fly backwards. *I* can fly backwards,' said Humming Bird. 'And now I shall tell you ...'

'Her-grok-grak,' sang the yellow frogs. 'Frogs can't fly. Backwards *or* forwards! Her-grok-grak. But frogs can sing.'

'Stop it. Stop it at once,' scolded Humming Bird. 'How can the parrots hear what I say, if you make that horrible noise while I'm speaking?'

Humming Bird beat her wings, and flew backwards.

'Squawk,' said the parrots. 'Squawk. How clever!'

Hop-step-kick danced the yellow frogs. 'We can *dance* backwards.' Hop-step-kick.

'Squawk,' said the parrots. 'Squawk. *Very* clever!'

'Stop it, frogs,' scolded Humming Bird. 'If you can't keep still, then go away. I want the parrots to look at *me*.'

The four little frogs crept sadly away.

'The sun will soon go down,' they said. 'This beautiful day will be gone for ever. Yet no one will let us sing or dance. We suppose we must sit beneath this tree, and not say a word, and keep very still, and be miserable until bedtime.'

'Tu-whoo. Who are you?' said a voice above them.

The four little frogs looked up at the tree. They saw Spectacled Owl and her fluffy white owlet sitting

143

side by side on a branch. Little white Owlet was fast asleep.

'Tu-whoo,' said Mrs Spectacled Owl. 'Tu-whoo. Who are you? Do you hoot, little creatures?'

'No,' said the yellow frogs. 'We sing.'

'Good!' said Mrs Spectacled Owl; and the frogs were so surprised that they stared. 'Good! Then sing. Very loudly, please. It's time little owlets were wide awake, but *this* little owlet won't open his eyes.'

'But isn't it bedtime, Mrs Owl?' said the four little yellow jungle frogs.

'Bedtime!' said Mrs Spectacled Owl. 'Of course not! It's night time. Time to get up.'

'*We* go to sleep in the night,' said the frogs.

'Do you?' said Mrs Spectacled Owl. 'You must be very peculiar creatures.'

'Her-grok-grak,' sang the little yellow frogs. 'Her-grok-grak. Wake up, little Owlet.'

'Can't you sing louder?' said Mrs Owl.

'Of course we can,' said the yellow frogs, and they sang and sang, at the tops of their voices.

'Her-grok-grak. What a beautiful day. Her-grok-grak. Oh *now* we feel happy.'

Little white Owlet opened his eyes. Then he sighed, and tried to sleep again.

'Do something new,' hooted Mrs Owl. 'Don't let my owlet sleep again.'

The four little frogs danced and danced. Hop-step-kick. Faster and faster. Hop-step-kick. Higher and higher.

'Whoo-hoo-hoo,' said little white Owlet, and his eyes opened wide as he stared at the frogs.

'Good!' said Mrs Spectacled Owl. 'My owlet is wide awake at last. Thank you, peculiar little creatures. You sing very loudly. You dance very well.'

Then away she flew, with her owlet beside her.

'Her-grok-grak,' sang the yellow frogs, as the sun went down behind the trees. 'Her-grok-grak. We sing very loudly.'

Hop-step-kick. Away they danced. Hop-step-kick. Home to their beds.

Red Umbrella and Yellow Scarf

MONKEY put on his yellow scarf.

'It is warm today,' said Marmoset. 'That yellow scarf is useless, Monkey.'

Monkey opened his red umbrella and held it high above his head.

'It is dry today,' said Marmoset. 'That red umbrella is useless, Monkey.'

Monkey did not say a word. He smiled, and walked

away through the jungle, his yellow scarf around his neck, his red umbrella above his head.

He came to a stream and saw Jacana. Jacana Bird stepped along on the bank, and her five little chicks bobbed and scuttled behind her, black and golden, like bumble bees.

Mother Jacana turned her head, fluttering yellow wings at the chicks.

'Now we must cross the stream,' she said. 'You are far too fluffy and small for swimming. Here is a pathway of lily-pad leaves. Walk carefully, chicks. The water is deep.'

The shiny round leaves lay still on the water, making a pathway from bank to bank. Jacana stepped on a lily-pad, spreading out her long, thin toes. 'Come,' she called. 'This leaf is safe.'

The five little chicks hopped on the leaf, and cheeped as it dipped and swayed beneath them.

Mother Jacana stepped to the next leaf.

'Come,' she called. '*This* leaf is safe.' And the five little chicks scuttled behind her.

Now they were half-way across the stream.

'Come,' called Mother Jacana again.

Four little chicks scuttled behind her. The last one stood still, looking at a lily bud.

'Why have you closed yourself up?' he asked. 'What are you hiding inside you, lily bud?'

He pushed his beak between the petals and wriggled his head inside the bud. And he found himself staring into the eyes of the biggest brown bee he had ever seen.

'Buzz!' went the bee. The chick fell backwards and slid across the lily-pad, splashing in the stream among the little silver bubbles.

Monkey did not have a boat. But he had his scarf, and he had his umbrella. He turned the umbrella upside down, so that it floated on the water. He tied on the yellow scarf for a sail. Then he sat in his red umbrella-boat, and sailed down the stream to Jacana chick. He lifted him gently out of the water, and set him down on the lily-pad. Jacana chick jumped up and down on the leaf, shaking the water out of his fluff. Then he bobbed and scuttled after his mother. When mother Jacana turned around, there were five little chicks on the leaf behind her.

'Come,' she said. 'We have reached the bank.'

Monkey walked away from the stream, his yellow scarf around his neck, his red umbrella above his head. He came to a cliff, and sat down to rest. He heard a little snuffling sound, and leaned out over the cliff to look. A soft, round, golden-brown creature was clinging to a creeper rope. She lifted her small furry face to Monkey, staring with unhappy eyes.

'Be careful, Little Opossum,' called Monkey. 'Don't fall on to those rocks below.'

Little Opossum started to climb, clinging tightly with her claws, moving up and up the creeper until she was close to the top of the cliff. Monkey stretched out a paw to help her.

Snap! The creeper broke in half!

'Oh-ee-ee!' cried Little Opossum. Down she fell to the rocks below.

Monkey did not have a ladder. But he had his scarf, and he had his umbrella. He turned the umbrella upside down and tied it to the yellow scarf. Then he lay on the grass at the edge of the cliff and gently lowered the red umbrella until it rested by Little Opossum.

Little Opossum sat in the umbrella. It rocked as Monkey pulled it up, and Little Opossum hid her face in her paws.

'You are safe,' said Monkey. 'Open your eyes.'

Little Opossum climbed from the umbrella, and trotted happily over the grass.

Monkey walked away from the cliff, his yellow scarf around his neck, his red umbrella above his head. He went to the mud flats and sat on a shell bank. He shaded his eyes from the sun with his paw, and looked across at the mangrove trees standing on tangled roots in the mud. Among the roots sat angry red crabs, guarding the doors of their tunnel homes. The crabs that sat in the branches above were thin and grey, with bright red claws. They stared at the screeching yellow parrots busily flying from tree to tree.

Then Monkey saw Turtle. Poor old Turtle was trying to find his way to the shell bank. He was old and tired, and he seemed to be lost as he plodded along by the mangrove trees.

'Keep away, keep away!' called the angry red crabs.

'Get out, get out!' screamed the thin grey crabs.

'Chase him away!' screeched the yellow parrots.

Turtle did not know where to turn.

'This way, Turtle,' Monkey called.

Turtle turned towards the shell bank. The angry red crabs, the thin grey crabs, and the screeching parrots pinched him and bit him, and chased him over the mud to the shell bank. There they turned him on his back, and left him in the hot sun.

'Poor old Turtle,' Monkey said. He put out a paw and lifted old Turtle, setting him gently on to his legs. But Turtle could not move away. The sun was

151

too hot, and his feet were too sore. He wanted to sleep until he felt better.

Monkey did not have a bed. But he had his scarf, and he had his umbrella.

He folded the scarf to make a bed, and stood the umbrella beside it, for shade. Then he lifted poor old Turtle again, and put him down on the yellow bed. Turtle sighed, and closed his eyes.

When the sun went down behind the mangroves, Turtle smiled, and stretched his legs. Then he stumped away happily home to his supper.

'And I must go home to *my* supper,' said Monkey.

He smiled to himself as he walked away, his yellow scarf around his neck, his red umbrella above his head.

As soon as he reached his tree in the jungle, he took off his scarf and folded it neatly.

'It was warm today,' said Marmoset. 'That yellow scarf was useless, Monkey.'

Monkey closed the red umbrella and hung it carefully over a branch.

'It was dry today,' said Marmoset. 'That red umbrella was useless, Monkey.'

Monkey did not say a word. Later, perhaps, he would tell Marmoset. But now it was time for his supper.

Armadillo Rescues Sloth

'Look! Here's a footprint,' said Armadillo. Sloth shook the hair away from his eyes as he hung upside down from a branch of his tree. He stared down at gentle Armadillo, whose neat round body was dressed in armour.

'Where?' he asked. 'Where is the footprint?'

'Here, on the ground,' said Armadillo. 'The tall white hunter has walked this way. He has left the print of his boot on the ground.'

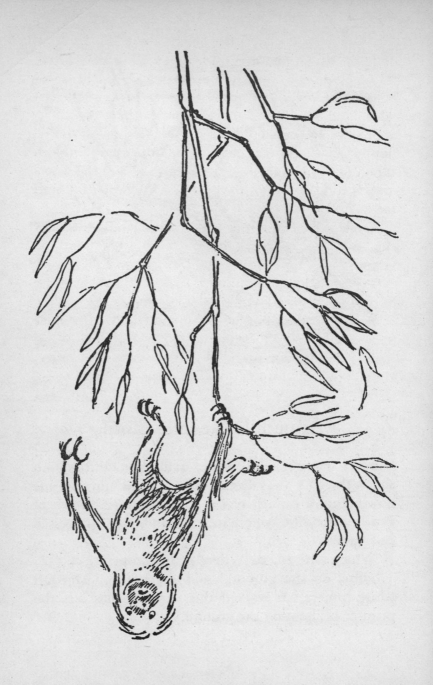

'I am made for an upside-down life,' said Sloth. 'My legs are for hanging, not for walking. But never before and never again shall I see the print of the tall white hunter, and so I must see it now.'

Slowly, he hooked his way to the ground, and flopped flat on the grass. Armadillo stared. Sloth raised his chin from the grass, and said: 'I am *not* a creature that walks on the ground. My legs won't hold me up, you see.'

Armadillo started to laugh. 'You look like a hairy rug,' he said. 'Oh, he he! A hairy rug!' And he laughed so much that he rolled in the grass.

'It is *not* a laughing matter,' said Sloth. 'What if the hunter should come back and find me?'

Armadillo stared at Sloth, and Sloth stared back as they heard heavy footsteps. The hunter! 'Run, Armadillo!' hissed Sloth. But Armadillo was brave. He stayed. The hunter took no notice of him, being far too busy staring at Sloth. He prodded Sloth with a big black boot.

'A rug is no use in the jungle,' he said. 'But it's just what I need for my house. So I'll take it. Whenever my feet feel tired, after hunting, I'll stand on my beautiful hairy rug.'

'No!' squeaked Sloth and Armadillo.

But the hunter had gone to get a rope. He tied it around Sloth's neck, then he pulled. He pulled poor Sloth through the door of his house, and put him down on the floor, by the window. Then he went out hunting again.

Sloth's little eyes were red with anger.

He hooked his claws in the floorboards, and pulled. His body moved an inch or two. He hooked, and pulled, and moved again.

'Hsst!' said a voice, and Armadillo poked his head around the door. 'Hsst! It's this way, Sloth,' he whispered.

Hook and pull, hook and pull; Sloth worked hard. Armadillo pushed. Sloth had almost reached the door when Armadillo heard heavy footsteps. He scampered behind a chair to hide.

In strode the hunter.

'Ah!' he said. 'Now I can stand on my nice new rug.'

He marched through the doorway and tripped over Sloth. He looked at the window; he looked at Sloth.

'A rug that *walks!*' he said to himself. 'Well, well, well! What a wonderful thing! I must put it into a cage at once. At the end of the day I will pack it up and send it to London for people to look at. They'll think I'm a very good hunter indeed when they see my wonderful walking rug.'

'I *won't* be a walking rug,' said Sloth. But the hunter had gone to get the rope. He tied it round Sloth's neck, then he pulled. He pulled poor Sloth to a cage in the clearing. He slammed the cage door and walked away.

Sloth thumped his stump of a tail on the ground.

'I don't want to go to London,' he said. 'I want to stay in my nice safe jungle.'

'Poor old Sloth,' said Armadillo. 'I'll open the door

and let you out. Then you can hook and pull to your tree.'

'I can't hook and pull on the ground,' wailed Sloth. 'My claws wouldn't hook; they would slip through the grass.'

'Oh! What a nuisance!' sighed Armadillo. 'Well, first we must let you out of your cage, and then we must think of another way to get you back to your own safe tree.'

He started to tug at the door of the cage.

But the hunter had not gone far when he thought: 'I don't want my walking rug to escape. Jaguar must guard it for me.'

Armadillo scampered away as big yellow Jaguar came to the clearing. Jaguar ran to the cage and sat down.

Armadillo sat by a tree and stared at Jaguar. Jaguar growled.

'I wish I were bigger,' sighed Armadillo. He sighed again, and started to think.

A little later Armadillo waddled away on his fat stumpy legs. Armadillo had thought of a plan. He went to the bush where the soldier ants worked.

'Please, good Soldier Ants,' he pleaded. 'Come and help me to rescue Sloth.'

The little black ants ran here and there, taking no notice of Armadillo.

'Please, kind Soldier Ants,' begged Armadillo. 'I know you are busy, but Sloth is in trouble.'

The little black ants ran faster than ever. They did not look at Armadillo. It seemed as though they did not hear him.

'They are *soldier* ants,' thought Armadillo. He waddled away behind a rock, picked up a tuft of soft green grass, and polished his armour until it shone. He held up his head and marched along smartly back to the bush, where the ants were working.

'Soldier Ants!' he shouted. 'Attention!'

The little black ants stood perfectly still.

'Soldier Ants!' Armadillo shouted. 'March to the ground and line up in threes.'

The ants marched down to the ground and stood there, a long black army, three in a row.

'Soldier Ants!' shouted Armadillo. 'Quick march! Left right, left right, left!'

Off went the army of ants through the jungle, their little black legs in perfect step.

'Left right, left!' panted Armadillo, marching behind in his shining armour.

The long black army of marching ants came to the clearing.

Jaguar blinked. But was he afraid of ants? Not he. He was a Jaguar, strongest beast in the jungle!

The ants were an inch from Jaguar's paws.

Armadillo drew himself up.

'Soldier Ants!' he shouted. 'Attack!'

The ants ran all over Jaguar's body. They burrowed beneath his fur and bit him. They bit him and nipped him in so many places that Jaguar jumped up, crying with pain, and ran away howling into the jungle.

At first, Sloth laughed. But then he remembered that somehow he had to get back to his tree.

Armadillo opened the cage door.

'What is the use of that?' grumbled Sloth.

But Armadillo had disappeared. He passed Sloth's tree and walked through the jungle, dragging the rope that had tied up Sloth. He had not gone far, when, between the trees, he saw Jaguar sitting beside the river.

Jaguar slapped and flapped with his paws, trying to drive away some ants that were still in hiding beneath his fur.

Armadillo's short fat legs shook beneath him, but bravely he called: 'Jaguar, why are you slapping and flapping?'

Jaguar did not want to say that the tiny ants were annoying him. He flapped his paws again, and said: 'I am exercising my legs, of course. I am Jaguar, strongest beast in the jungle. And why am I strong? I will tell you why. It's because I do my exercises.'

Armadillo jumped up and down.

'Why are you jumping?' Jaguar asked.

Armadillo panted for breath.

'I am doing *my* exercises,' he said. 'I am very strong as well.'

'Oh, ho ho!' Jaguar laughed. 'Let's have a tug-of-war, little boaster. One pull from me, and before you

can sneeze, you'll be splashing about in that river behind me.'

'Here is a rope,' said Armadillo. 'Tie one end of it
round your middle.'

Jaguar tied the rope, and he laughed.

'The rope is long,' said Armadillo. 'I'll carry my
end of it back through the trees to stretch it out
straight. When I'm ready I'll call you.'

Armadillo held the rope, and dragged his end of it
back to the clearing. Quickly he tied it round Sloth's
neck.

'Are you ready to pull?' Jaguar called. 'One, two, three. Go!' And he pulled on the rope.

Sloth moved slowly out of the cage on the other end of the long rope.

'H'm, that's funny!' Jaguar said. 'I thought I could pull Armadillo easily.'

He leaned back and pulled again on the rope.

Sloth moved half-way across the clearing.

Jaguar stood by the river bank, pulling and pulling until he was tired.

Sloth was pulled to the trunk of his tree.

'Jaguar!' Armadillo called. 'Please stop pulling just for a minute. The knot on my end of the rope has worked loose. I must tie it before we start pulling again.'

Jaguar was glad to rest. He shut his eyes and gathered his strength. Armadillo untied the knot that held the rope around Sloth's neck. Sloth climbed into his own safe tree and hooked himself upside down on a branch.

Jaguar gathered himself together. Now he would pull as never before.

'One, two, three. Pull!' called Armadillo, and he dropped the end of the rope, and waited.

Jaguar gave a mighty pull. The rope flew up in the air. So did Jaguar. Head over heels into the river!

Sloth yawned widely and opened his eyes. 'I thought I heard a splash,' he said. 'Did *you* hear a very big splash, Armadillo?'

When Armadillo stopped laughing, he said: 'Are you wanting to know what that splash was, Sloth?'

Sloth stared up at his own hooking claws.

'Never, never, never again shall I come down out of my tree,' he said. 'I do not care about the splash. And if you should happen to see a footprint, kindly do not mention it.'

Armadillo smiled to himself. And never again did he see the footprint of the tall white hunter. For when the hunter came back to the clearing and saw that his walking rug had escaped, he was so annoyed that he packed up his things, left the jungle, and went home to London.

Armadillo heard him go. And Armadillo stretched his legs, rolled himself up in his shining armour, and went to sleep with a smile on his face.

Pig Says Positive

MONKEY sat in a coconut tree. Below, on the ground, sat Peccary Pig.

'Pig, will it rain today?' asked Monkey. 'I want to go to the jungle clearing, to plant a coconut under the ground. But I can't plant my coconut today unless there is rain to make it grow.'

'Rain?' said Peccary Pig. 'It might.'

Monkey picked a coconut, and ran through the jungle with it, singing:

'Pig says might, pig says might,
Shut the door and bolt it tight.'

When Monkey came to the grassland, he met a creature with short black legs, a black bushy tail, and a fat brown body.

'Hello, Sausage,' Monkey called.

The creature said: 'I'm Bush Dog, not Sausage. Where are you taking that coconut?'

'I'm going to plant it,' Monkey told him.

'What a waste of good food; let's eat it,' said Bush Dog.

Monkey looked up into the sky. There was only one small ragged raincloud.

'Very well,' he agreed. 'We'll share it.'

'First we must roast it,' Bush Dog said. 'Go away and find some firewood, and I will guard the coconut.'

Monkey put the coconut down, and went away to find the firewood. When he came back, Bush Dog was smiling, and Bush Dog was full of coconut. Lying behind him were two empty shells.

'You have eaten my coconut,' Monkey shouted.

He threw the empty shells at Bush Dog.

'Sausage!' he shouted. And he ran through the jungle, back to his tree.

'Pig, do you *know* it will rain?' he asked.

'Know?' said Peccary Pig. 'Yes, I know. I can smell it in the air. That's proof.'

Monkey picked another coconut, and ran through the jungle with it, singing:

'Pig says proof, pig says proof,
Shut the door and mend the roof.'

When Monkey came to the swampy land, he met a

creature without a tail. His back legs were short and his front legs were long. He had shaggy brown fur and sharp curving teeth.

'Hello, Fatty,' Monkey called.

'I'm Capybara,' the creature said. 'Where are you taking that coconut?'

'I'm going to plant it,' Monkey told him.

'I think that's silly,' said Capybara. 'Coconuts are good to eat.'

Monkey looked up into the sky. There were two black rainclouds. 'We'll share it,' he said.

Capybara looked at the coconut. Then he looked at Monkey's paws.

'You must wash your paws before dinner,' he said. 'They are muddy. Go to the lake and wash them. I will guard the coconut.'

Monkey went to wash his paws. When he came back, Capybara was smiling, and Capybara was rubbing his tummy. In the mud beside him lay two empty shells.

'*Your* paws were muddy too,' shouted Monkey.

He threw the shells at Capybara.

'Fatty!' he shouted. And he ran through the jungle back to his tree.

'Pig, will it rain quite soon?' he asked.

'Soon?' said Peccary Pig. 'Yes, I'm certain.'

Monkey picked a third coconut, and ran through the jungle with it, singing:

'Pig says certain, pig says certain,
Shut the door and draw the curtain.'

166

When Monkey reached the river shell bank, he met a creature with smooth grey fur, a long bushy tail with rings around it, and paws that were very large and flat.

'Hello, Flattypaws,' said Monkey.

'I'm Crab-eater Raccoon,' the creature said. 'Where are you taking that coconut?'

'I'm going to plant it,' Monkey told him.

'Plant it?' said Raccoon. 'How foolish! Let's eat it.'

Monkey looked at the thick black rainclouds, but one little patch of sky was blue.

'Yes, we'll share it. Half each!' he said. 'I shall *not* go away to gather firewood. I shall *not* go away to wash my paws. I shall stay where I am, on this shell bank.'

'Of course you will,' said Crab-eater Raccoon. 'We must split the coconut in half.'

Raccoon lifted his large flat paw and patted the coconut, pat-pat-pat.

'Why are you patting?' Monkey asked.

'I want to break the shell,' said Raccoon. 'I often eat crabs, and *they* have shells. I pat-pat-pat, and pat-pat-pat, until the crab feels dreadfully tired. Then I can easily break its shell.'

'Silly Raccoon!' Monkey laughed. 'You can't make a coconut feel tired.'

'In that case,' said Raccoon. 'It's no use to pat. You must climb to the top of a tall tree, and drop the coconut on to a stone.'

'I shall *not* go away to a tree,' said Monkey. 'I shall stay where I am, on this shell bank.'

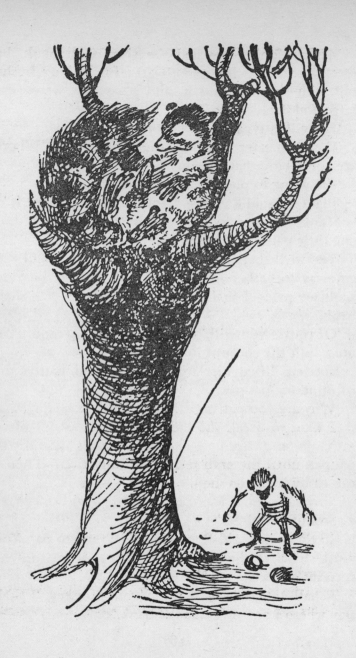

'Just as you please,' said Crab-eater Raccoon. He took the coconut, went to a tree, climbed to the top, and sat on a branch.

Monkey sat on the shell bank, and waited.

He waited for quite a long time on that shell bank.

At last he called: 'Hurry up, Raccoon. Drop the coconut on to the stone.'

Out of the tree fell two empty shells. When Monkey looked up into the tree, Raccoon was smiling, and Raccoon was full.

'Greedy old Flattypaws!' Monkey shouted. And he ran through the jungle, back to his tree.

'Pig, are you sure it will rain?' he asked.

'Sure?' said Peccary Pig. 'I'm positive.'

Monkey picked a fourth coconut, and ran through the jungle with it, singing:

> 'Pig says positive, pig says positive,
> Shut the door and . . .'

Monkey stopped. He could not think of a rhyme. He ran on through the jungle, singing:

> 'Pig says positive, pig says positive,
> Pig says positive, hositive, fositive . . .'

He looked around for someone to help him. But the creatures knew that the rain was coming. They had gone to their homes.

Monkey reached the jungle clearing. The sky was quite covered by big black rainclouds, but Monkey did not notice them. He did not plant his coconut.

169

The only thing that mattered to Monkey was finding a rhyme. So he tried again:

'Pig says positive, pig says positive,
Pig says positive, lositive, wositive ...'

Drops of rain fell on his head. Plop!
'Goodness, I'm getting wet,' said Monkey.
Back across the jungle he ran, home to his tree. Below the tree, Peccary Pig still sat on the ground.
Monkey climbed to a branch where the rain could not reach him. He split the coconut in half, and ate the sweet white middle of it. Only the two empty shells were left.

He threw one down, and it bounced off Pig's head and fell in the grass.

'It's a hat,' called Monkey. 'I knew it would rain, so I made two hats. And that one is yours.'

Pig and Monkey put on their hats. Pig hummed the tune as Monkey sang:

'Pig says positive, pig has a hat,
There's the rhyme, so that is that.'

Monkey felt happy. He smiled at Pig. Pig smiled back, and hummed the tune.

What Does It Matter?

THE mother creatures said to their babies:

'Now you must learn to say three things: your name, and the name of the place where you live, and the name of the thing that you eat for your supper.'

'Why must we learn all that?' asked the babies.

'To keep you safe!' said the mother creatures. 'Babies wander, and lose their way. If you know your name, and the place where you live, and the thing that you like to eat for your supper, you'll never get lost and you'll never go hungry.'

'We like to be safe. We will learn,' said the babies.

Capybara Baby started.

'I'm Capybara Baby,' he said. 'I live in a swamp. I eat green things.'

Little Red Ibis Bird flapped his wings.

'I'm Ibis Baby. I live on the mud flats. I eat little shiny fish for my supper.'

Pimpla Hog said: 'I'm Pimpla Hog Baby. I live in a tree. I eat fruit, and nuts.'

Spectacled Owl Baby said: 'I'm Owlet. I live near the stream. I eat shrimps.'

Anteater Baby said. 'Fonk, fonk, fonk! I'm Anteater Baby. I live on the grasslands. I like to eat ants for my supper. Fonk!'

'Good,' said the mother creatures. 'Good.'

'Now it is your turn,' said Mother Sloth to her baby. 'You are Baby Sloth. You live in a tree. You eat cecropia leaves for your supper.'

Sloth Baby said: 'I want to sleep. And why must I say that difficult word? What does it matter? I never wander. I can't get lost. So what does it matter?'

Mother Sloth sighed. 'You naughty baby! You never know *what* might happen,' she said. 'And if you were lost, *I* couldn't find you! Nor could your father. We're Sloths. We don't walk.'

'That's what I said,' yawned Sloth Baby rudely. 'I can't leave my tree, so I'll never get lost. So what does it matter? Not at all!'

And he curled himself into a fuzzy grey bundle.

'Your father will spank you,' Mother Sloth scolded. 'I'll find him and tell him how naughty you are.'

Sloth Baby's head was filling with dreams, when suddenly along came Monkey, with a bucket. He put it down beneath the tree. Clash, clang, bang!

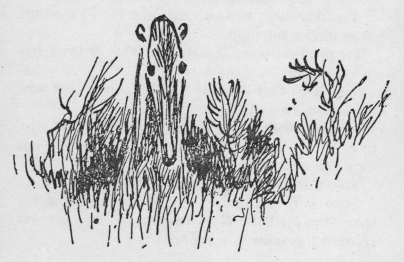

Sloth Baby wriggled.

'I'm sleeping,' he grumbled.

Monkey danced around the bucket. 'A bucket, a bucket, a shiny big bucket!' he sang. 'I'll carry it, sail in it, jump on it, rattle it. Then I will bang on it. Clash, clang, bang! But first I will leave it beneath this tree while I go through the jungle to get my dinner.'

'Bother!' said Sloth Baby. 'How can I sleep? I suppose I must go to a quieter place.'

He clung upside down to a branch of the tree.

'Now I must move, I suppose,' he said.

One of his back legs waved in the air; it was much too lazy to reach the branch.

'What does it matter?' Sloth Baby said. 'Three of my legs are still holding me on.'

His other back leg waved in the air. It could not reach the branch; it was lazy.

'What does it matter?' Sloth Baby said. 'Two of my legs are still holding me on.'

One of his front legs waved in the air. It was lazy; it could not reach the branch.

'What does it matter?' Sloth Baby said. 'One of my legs is still holding me on.'

His other front leg waved in the air. *None* of his legs was holding him on.

Bang! Clang! He fell in the bucket!

'Oh well!' he said. 'Now that I'm here I will rest for a minute.'

One minute passed. Sloth Baby rested.

Five minutes passed. Sloth Baby yawned.

Ten minutes passed. Sloth Baby slept.

Cecropia flowers fell from the tree and covered him up with their soft warm petals. Sloth Baby dreamed quiet dreams beneath them.

Monkey came back. He picked up the bucket.

'Goodness! It's full of flowers,' he said. 'I'll carry my bucket down to the mud flats, and wait for the tide to come in from the sea. Then I will throw all these flowers in the water, and sail in my bucket. That's what I'll do.'

He carried the bucket across the jungle. Sloth Baby woke, and squealed with fright.

'My bucket is squeaking,' Monkey said.

He reached the mud flats, and sat down to wait.

'There isn't a river yet,' he said. 'But there *will* be a river, as soon as the water comes in from the sea. And when it is deep, I'll sail in my bucket.'

'Let me get out,' Sloth Baby cried. 'I want to go home. Let me get out.'

'Help!' said Monkey. 'My bucket is talking. I'll throw it away before it can harm me.'

He threw it away, plop-squelch, in the mud.

'Now you are stuck, talking bucket,' he said. 'The tide will come in and the water will drown you.'

Sloth Baby wriggled his fuzzy grey head over the rim of the bucket, and called: 'Let me get out. *I* shall drown too.'

But Monkey had run back into the jungle.

Sloth Baby heard the lap-lap-lap, as the water came in from the grey sea. It slapped at the sides of the bucket.

'Oh, help me. Don't let me drown!' Sloth Baby cried.

In with the tide came the Anableps Fish.

Each little Anableps looked in the air, using the tops of his two-piece eyes. With the bottom halves of his two-piece eyes, each little Anableps looked in the water. Anableps Fish always saw *everything*.

That is why they saw the bucket.

They saw a fuzzy grey head as well.

'Are you a new kind of fish?' they asked.

'No,' wailed Sloth Baby. 'Water is horrid. Water will drown me. I want to go home.'

'Well,' said the Anableps. 'Crocodile *might* help.'

'Ask him to save me,' Baby Sloth pleaded.

The Anableps stared unkindly, and said: 'We move with the tide, and the tide moves slowly. Crocodile lives far, far up the river.'

'Please go and fetch him,' Sloth Baby pleaded.

The Anableps Fish started to move. As each little wave of the incoming tide filled the muddy ditches with water, each little Anableps slid to a puddle. They swam around and around in the puddle, waiting for water to fill up the next ditch.

Sloth Baby cried: 'You move so slowly. Don't let me drown. Fetch Crocodile quickly.'

The Anableps slid from puddle to puddle, until they were out of sight up the river. Then Sloth Baby cried. He was all alone. He hid beneath the cecropia petals.

Just as the sky began to darken, Crocodile swam

down the river, searching, turning his head from side to side.

Sloth Baby jumped up and down in the bucket.

'Here! Mr Crocodile, here I am.'

Just as the sun began to set, Crocodile swam up the river again, carrying Baby Sloth in the bucket. Sloth Baby's little red eyes grew wide as he watched the water rushing by. Crocodile set him down on the bank.

The mother creatures gathered around, looking at Sloth as he sat in the bucket, and saying: 'Poor little baby creature. What is your name? We will take you home.'

Sloth Baby grunted, and wrinkled his nose.

'My name is ... my name is ... I don't remember.'

'Where do you live?' asked the mother creatures.

'I live in a ...'

'Swamp?' asked Capybara.

'On the mud flats?' Red Ibis flapped her wings.

'In a tree?' asked Pimpla Hog.

'Stream?' asked Owl.

'Fonk! the grasslands?' Anteater grunted.

'No,' said Baby Sloth. 'No, I don't think so.' The mother creatures looked at him sternly.

'How can we take you home?' they said. 'You ought to have learned where you live, baby creature.'

'Ha!' said Crocodile. 'What does it matter? When Jaguar sees him, he'll gobble him up.'

Sloth Baby cried. But he could not remember.

'He is hungry,' the mother creatures said. 'We'll get him some supper. Now, what do you eat?'

Sloth Baby wailed. But he could not remember.
Capybara brought him green things.
Ibis brought him little shiny fish.
Pimpla Hog brought him fruits, and nuts.

Owl brought him shrimps; Anteater brought him ants.

But Sloth Baby wailed, and shook his head.

'What can we do?' said the mother creatures. 'You ought to have learned what you eat, baby creature.'

'Ha!' said Crocodile. 'What does it matter? He'll get thinner and thinner until he is nothing.'

Sloth Baby's eyes grew wide and frightened. He hid beneath the cecropia petals.

'Where has he gone?' asked Capybara.

'Beneath the petals,' Red Ibis said.

Pimpla Hog said: 'What *are* those petals? He brought them with him. They come from his home. I wish that we knew the name of those petals.'

'Then we should know where he lives,' said Owl.

'Fonk!' said Anteater. '*I* don't know them. I am a creature that stays on the grasslands. Who goes everywhere? Who would know?'

'Monkey goes everywhere,' Crocodile said. 'Monkey! We want you. Come at once.'

Monkey turned pale when he saw the bucket.

'This is the bucket that talks,' he said.

'Nonsense!' said Crocodile. 'Look inside it. Tell us the name of those petals, Monkey.'

'Those are cecropia petals,' said Monkey.

Sloth Baby's fuzzy grey head appeared. He smiled at the mother creatures, and said: 'Now I remember that difficult word. I am Baby Sloth, and I live in a tree, and I eat cecropia leaves for my supper.'

'Take him, Monkey,' Crocodile said. 'He's a bad little nuisance. Take him home.'

Monkey ran across the jungle, shaking Baby Sloth in the bucket. But Sloth Baby smiled. He was going home.

Monkey reached the cecropia tree, and turned the bucket upside down. Out, in a shower of petals, fell Sloth Baby. Monkey ran through the jungle again, clanging and banging his shiny bucket.

Sloth Baby climbed up into the tree, and his mother and father grunted for joy. They scolded him, hugged him, spanked him, and kissed him.

Sloth Baby smiled.

He was home. He was safe.

Peccary Piglet's Collar

PECCARY PIGLET was very unhappy. All his big brothers had neat white collars. Peccary Piglet was black all over.

'Why can't I have a white collar?' he shouted, '*Why* can't I have a white collar? I want one.'

'Wait!' his elder brothers smiled. 'You are only a *small* Peccary Piglet. Therefore it is right that you are black all over. When you grow older, you will also grow a collar.'

But Peccary wanted a collar at once.

He picked a palm leaf, and said to himself: 'It's a very good palm leaf for keeping the rain off. I'll sell it to someone who'll give me a collar.'

Off through the jungle he ran with the palm leaf.

'I should like it,' Jaguar said. 'But I want it for keeping off flies, not rain. I'll pay you with one of my smart black spots.'

Jaguar flicked at flies with the palm leaf, and Peccary went away with the spot.

'Who will buy my spot?' he called. 'It's big and black and very smart.'

'I should like it,' said Coatimundi. 'But I don't want to wear it. I want it to sit on. The ground near the river is dreadfully damp. I'll pay you with this big brown nut.'

Coatimundi sat on the spot, and Peccary went away with the nut.

'Who will buy this nut?' he called. 'It's big and brown, and nice to eat.'

'I should like it,' said Pimpla Hog Porcupine. 'But not for eating! For throwing and catching! I'll pay you with one of my sharp spines.'

Pimpla Hog threw the nut, and caught it, and Peccary went away with the spine.

'Who wants to buy a sharp spine?' he called. 'It's a very good spear for keeping you safe.'

'I should like it,' Pelican said. 'But not for a spear. For combing myself! I'll pay you with one of my big white feathers.'

Pelican combed herself with the spine, and Peccary went away with the feather.

'Who wants to buy a feather?' he called. 'It comes from a bird that can swim in the water.'

'I should like it,' Crocodile said. 'But I don't want to use it for swimming, of course. I want it to shade my eyes from the sun. I'll pay you with one of these bones from my dinner.

'No,' said Peccary. 'Pay me with a collar.'

'What is a collar?' Crocodile asked. 'This bone is the only thing that I have. Unless you would care for a tooth from my head. I can soon grow a new one. I often do it.'

'Give the bone *and* the tooth,' said Peccary.

Crocodile lay on the bank to rest, shading his eyes from the sun with the feather, and Peccary took the bone and the tooth.

Before he could say that he wanted to sell them, along came Hunter's Dog, panting for breath. And Peccary nearly danced for joy when he saw that around Dog's neck was a collar, a smart yellow collar with silver studs.

'A bone! I smell it! I want it!' said Dog. And he snatched the bone from Peccary's paws.

He scratched in the earth to dig a hole, meaning to bury the bone until tea-time.

'But the earth is so hard that I can't make the hole. A spade is what I need,' Dog grumbled.

'Here it is,' said Peccary Piglet, holding out Crocodile's tooth. 'Here's a spade.'

Dog tried to snatch it away from the piglet, but Peccary held on tightly, and said: 'I have given you the bone, and I'll sell you the spade. But what will you pay me for the spade, Hunter's Dog?'

'What *can* I pay you?' said Hunter's Dog. 'I can't spare my tail; I need it for wagging. I can't spare my nose; I need it for smelling. I can't spare my ears; I need them for hearing.'

'Pay me with the bone,' Peccary said.

Hunter's Dog howled with rage, and said: 'If I give you the bone to pay for the spade, I shan't need the spade to bury the bone.'

'Then you needn't have either,' said Peccary Piglet.

'What *can* I give you?' wailed Hunter's Dog.

Peccary Piglet pretended to think.

'I *could* take the collar you're wearing,' he said.

Hunter's Dog took off the yellow collar, and Peccary Piglet put it on.

Then he danced with delight.

He ran through the jungle towards his home, smiling, and wearing the yellow collar.

First he met Crocodile.

'Goodness!' said Crocodile. 'Pelican's feather is spoiling my eyes. It's making me see peculiar things, and I think I see Peccary wearing a collar. I don't want this feather that's spoiling my eyes. Take it away, Peccary Piglet.'

Peccary ran through the jungle again, with the yellow collar, and Pelican's feather.

Then he saw Pelican, combing herself.

'Oh!' said Pelican. 'What a surprise. Peccary Piglet is wearing a collar.'

Pelican did not think what she was doing because she was staring so hard at the piglet. She pricked herself with the sharp spine.

'Horrible, prickling spine!' she scolded. 'It hurt me. Take it away, I don't like it.'

Peccary set off for home again, with the yellow collar, and Pelican's feather, and Pimpla Hog's long, sharp spine.

Then he saw Pimpla Hog, throwing and catching the big brown nut.

'Throw!' said Pimpla Hog, tossing the nut.

'Oh!' said Pimpla Hog. 'What do I see? Peccary Piglet is wearing a collar.'

Then he forgot to catch the nut, and it fell on his head.

'Ee!' he squealed. 'Take it away. It hit me. I hate it.'

Peccary ran through the jungle again, with the yellow collar, and Pelican's feather, and Pimpla Hog's spine, and Coati's nut.

Then he saw Coati on Jaguar's spot.

'Help!' said Coatimundi. 'Help! I see a strange animal wearing a collar.' He jumped off the spot and ran away.

Peccary smiled as he ran through the jungle, with the yellow collar, the big white feather, the long sharp spine, the big brown nut, and the smart black spot.

Then he saw Jaguar, flicking at flies.

'I must be very tired,' said Jaguar. 'Only when Jaguars feel very tired do they see strange things. And I see one now. A piglet wearing a yellow collar! Perhaps it's this flicking that's making me tired. Take the palm leaf, Peccary Piglet. I'm much too tired to flick any more.'

Peccary Piglet went to his home. He sat down to rest on Jaguar's spot, flicking away the flies with the palm leaf, playing throw and catch with the nut, combing himself with the long sharp spine, shading his eyes from the sun with the feather, and proudly wearing the yellow collar.

When Peccary's brothers came back from the

jungle, they stared and stared at their little pig brother.

'Isn't he smart?' they said. 'Isn't he lucky? However did he get that yellow collar?'

Peccary Piglet smiled to himself. And he wore the collar, day and night, until he got bigger and grew his own.

The Chocolate Party

MONKEY had a barrel of chocolate.

There were bars of chocolate filled with toffee, bars of chocolate scrunchy with nuts, jelly babies in chocolate cradles, chocolate mice with string tails, and packets and packets of chocolate peppermint creams.

Monkey sat by his barrel and smiled.

Then along came Jaguar, looking for mischief.

'Chocolate, I see! Can I have some?' he asked.

'Not until sunset,' Monkey said. 'That's when I'm having my chocolate party. I'm going to ask all my friends to the party: Peccary Pig, and Capybara, the

Yellow Frogs, and Jacana Bird, Little Opossum and
Armadillo, and Marmoset, Crab-eater Raccoon, and
Turtle, and Coatimundi, and all the others. You can
come as well, if you would like to.'

Monkey ran across the jungle, to ask his friends to
the chocolate party.

When he came back, the barrel had gone.

'The sun was hot,' Jaguar said. 'I thought it would
melt your chocolate. So I buried the barrel beneath a
tree, to keep it safe for the chocolate party.'

'To keep it safe for Jaguar! That's what you really
mean,' said Monkey. 'Where have you hidden my
chocolate barrel? Is it beneath a coconut tree, or a
breadfruit tree, or another tree?'

Jaguar stroked his whiskers, and said: 'Riddle-me-ree, which is the tree? I'll tell you this. Its name has six letters. Crocodile knows the first letter. Anaconda knows the second. Pimpla Hog Porcupine knows the third. The Thrip Insect Babies know the fourth. Pelicans *may* remember the fifth. And Clever Young Turtle knows the sixth. But nobody knows the name of the tree. Except me!'

Monkey went to the wide brown river, where Crocodile rested on top of the water, smiling at nothing.

'What is the letter?' Monkey called.

Crocodile flicked his scaly tail. Then he swam to a place where a great green tree spread its branches over the water. Slowly, he opened his greedy mouth. And he fixed his little black eyes on Monkey.

'If you really want that letter,' he said. 'Ride on my back across the river.'

Monkey saw Crocodile's sharp white teeth that could easily bite a small monkey in half, and the mighty, scaly, beating tail that could break all the bones in a monkey's body.

'Catch me, and ride on my back,' called Crocodile. His great grey body shook with laughter.

Monkey found a creeper rope, and he tied one end of it into a loop. Then he climbed to the branch above Crocodile's head. He held the loop in his strong little paw, and suddenly sent it spinning downwards.

Snap! It closed around Crocodile's mouth.

Then Monkey jumped on to Crocodile's back, and pulled on the rope until Crocodile groaned, thinking that his neck would break.

'Swim!' shouted Monkey. 'Swim, you old Crocodile. Carry me across the river.'

Crocodile did as he was told.

Monkey jumped to the bank, and said: 'I shall set you free. Tell me the letter. If you play any tricks I shall catch you again.'

'The letter is B,' said Crocodile sulkily.

Monkey ran to the mangrove swamp, saying: 'Riddle-me-ree, the name of the tree begins with a B. Now I know the first letter, and Anaconda knows the second.'

Anaconda lay in the mud between the roots of a mangrove tree, sunning his grey-and-yellow back. Slowly he coiled up his long scaly body, and raised his head to look at Monkey.

'Anaconda!' Monkey called. 'Jaguar says that you know a letter.'

Anaconda's black eyes glittered.

'So that's what Jaguar said,' he hissed. 'But I shall say nothing, silly Monkey.'

'I'll tie you to a branch,' said Monkey.

Anaconda hissed with rage.

'You would need all the rope in the world,' he said. 'I'm as long as ... as long as ...' He raised his head. 'I'm as long as that mangrove branch above me.'

'I don't believe it,' Monkey said.

'I'll show you,' Anaconda told him. He glided up the trunk of the tree, and lay on the branch, stretching his body.

'You see! I said so!' he hissed at Monkey. 'My

head is touching the end of the branch, and my tail is touching the trunk. Can you see?'

'No,' said Monkey. 'I'll come up and look.'

He picked two stems of a creeper plant. Then he climbed up the trunk and stood on the branch, close to Anaconda's tail.

'Yes, your tail is touching the trunk,' he said. 'But I can't see your head. I will come out and look.'

He padded along the mangrove branch beside Anaconda's long, long body.

'Yes, your head's at the end of the branch,' he said. 'But now I am so far away from your tail that I can't see whether it's touching the trunk. I think you are cheating, Anaconda. You moved up the branch while I walked along it.'

'Nonsense!' Anaconda hissed. 'Tie my head to the end of the branch. Then you will know that I *can't* move along.'

Monkey took one creeper stem and tied Anaconda's head to the branch. He padded back to the trunk of the tree, and tied Anaconda's tail. Then he smiled.

'So now I have shown you,' said Anaconda. 'I *am* as long as the mangrove branch. You have tied me to it. You know I can't move.'

'Yes,' chuckled Monkey. 'I've tied you up.'

And he danced for joy on the mangrove branch.

Then he sat on Anaconda's back, and bounced up and down.

'Now tell me,' he said. 'I'll bounce on your back till you tell me the letter.'

'Stop it, stop it. The letter is A. You are hurting my back,' said Anaconda.

Monkey climbed to the ground, and called: 'Struggle and struggle until you break free.' And he ran to the edge of the jungle.

'Riddle-me-ree, the name of the tree is BA, and four more letters,' he said. 'Pimpla Hog Porcupine knows the next.'

Pimpla Hog sat in a tree, looking worried. He rattled his speckled grey spines at Monkey, and twitched his fat pink nose. Then he said: 'Something is tickling. It's very annoying.'

'I expect it's an ant in your spines,' said Monkey. 'Come down here, and I'll catch it for you.'

Pimpla Hog stood in front of Monkey, and Monkey searched among his spines. But the spines were sharp and they hurt Monkey's paws. He could not catch the tickling ant.

'Roll on the ground, and squash it,' said Monkey.

Pimpla Hog rolled on the ground. Then he twitched.

'The ant is still there. It's tickling,' he said.

'Do a good trick, and surprise it,' said Monkey.

Pimpla Hog stood on his hairy tail. Then he hit at the tail with a bunched up paw, so that he knocked himself on to the ground.

But his little black eyes filled with tears as he said: 'I *can't* get rid of that tickling ant.'

'Shake yourself hard,' Monkey told him.

Pimpla Hog shook till his face grew pink.

'Harder! Harder!' Monkey called.

Pimpla Hog shook till his spines rattled.

'Harder! Still harder!' Monkey called.

Pimpla Hog shook and shook and shook till his spines flew out and fell on the ground. And out flew the tickling ant as well.

'Ah!' sighed Pimpla Hog. 'That's better.'

Then he sneezed. 'I'm catching cold,' he said. 'And I'm easy to bite, without my spines. Help me to pick them up, please, Monkey, before I get eaten for somebody's dinner.'

'No!' said Monkey, folding his paws. 'Not unless you tell me the letter.'

Pimpla Hog rubbed his fat pink nose.

'I don't think I ought to tell you,' he said. 'Jaguar said that the letter was secret.'

'Jaguar played a trick,' Monkey told him. 'Jaguar hid my chocolate barrel. I can't have my chocolate party tonight unless I can find the name of the tree.'

'N,' said Pimpla Hog at once. 'The letter is N. Oh! That naughty Jaguar!'

Monkey helped him to gather the spines. Then he waved good-bye, and went to the grassland.

'Riddle-me-ree, the name of the tree is BAN,' he said to himself. 'And I hope that the Thrip babies know the next letter.'

Monkey found the Thrip babies playing, looking like little red shiny buttons. Four of them ran between the grass stalks, playing a game of Follow-the-leader.

Monkey spoke to the leading Thrip.

'Tell me the letter, Thrip,' he said.

The Thrip baby fell on his scarlet back and waved

his six tiny legs in the air. The other Thrips fell down on *their* scarlet backs, waving their eighteen legs in the air.

'Tell me the letter, Thrips,' called Monkey.

The leading Thrip hopped on three legs, and the other Thrips followed, hopping on nine legs.

'Tell me the letter at once,' shouted Monkey.

The leading Thrip stopped, and stared at Monkey. The other Thrips stopped and stared as well.

Monkey stooped to pick a grass stalk.

'If you don't say the letter, you naughty Thrips, I'll string you up on this grass stalk,' he said. 'I'll string you into a shiny red necklace, and wear you around my neck for ever.'

'I say A,' said the leading Thrip.

'We all say A,' said the other Thrips.

Monkey ran to the edge of the sea, saying: 'Riddle-me-ree, the name of the tree has BANA for its first four letters. Pelicans *may* remember the next.'

The pelicans wanted minnows for tea. Slowly, they swam out to sea, then they turned, facing the shore in a long white line. Then all at once they started to move, wading in towards the shore, wingtip to wingtip, their fat yellow beaks skimming the top of the grey sea. Now and again they beat the water, splashing it into foam with their wings. The frightened minnows swam before them, driven nearer and nearer the shore. They could not escape through the long white line.

Monkey stood on the shore and called: 'Pelicans, do you remember the letter?'

Only one pelican answered. He said: 'No, we don't remember, Monkey.'

'Ah!' said Monkey. 'You're Polite Pelican.'

The hungry pelicans stood near the shore, where the water was full of plump brown minnows. They opened their beaks and scooped up the fish.

Monkey looked at Polite Pelican.

Then he said: 'Good afternoon. I hope you are feeling well, Mr Pelican.'

Pelican's beak was full of fish. But, being polite, he had to answer: 'Good afternoon. I am quite well, thank you.'

Out of his beak jumped the wriggling fishes.

Pelican opened his beak very wide and scooped the minnows up again.

Monkey called: 'Good afternoon. Are you *sure* you are feeling well, Mr Pelican?'

Pelican sighed. He was very hungry. His pelican friends were eating fast. Before very long all the fish would be gone.

But, being polite, he had to answer: 'Good afternoon, I am sure I feel well.'

Out of his beak jumped the wriggling fishes.

Pelican watched them swimming away. It seemed he would never get his tea.

'Oh, good Mr Monkey,' he said. 'If you please, would you mind going away while I'm eating my tea? If you please!'

'I *could* go away at once,' said Monkey. 'I *could* go away, if I knew the letter.'

Pelican eyed the fish in the water.

'I think I've remembered, Monkey,' he said. 'The letter is N. Good afternoon.'

Monkey ran to the stream, saying: 'Riddle-me-ree, the name of the tree is BANAN. One more letter! Clever Young Turtle knows what it is.'

Turtle was taking a bath in a flower. He had hung his hard little shell on a bush, while he splashed in the water and scrubbed his back.

He sang to himself in a happy small voice:

> 'Rub a dub dub,
> If I can't find a tub
> Tra-la-lee,
> I wait for a shower
> To fill up a flower.
> Clever me!
> I splash and I splosh
> While I'm having my wash,
> Tra-la-la
> Tra-la-la
> Tra-la-lee.'

'Oh Clever Young Turtle!' Monkey called.

Turtle's little black eyes appeared over the top of the scarlet flower.

'I'm bathing,' he said. 'Go away.'

'What is the letter?' Monkey asked.

Splash! went Turtle, back in his bath.

'I'll take away your shell,' said Monkey.

'In that case, I'll tell you,' said Turtle at once. 'But how can I think, while you stare at me so? Shut your eyes and count to ten. Then I will try to remember the letter.'

As soon as Monkey started to count, Clever Young Turtle jumped from his bath, and crept on the tips of his toes to his shell.

But Monkey counted very quickly.

'Eight, nine, ten!' He opened his eyes, and saw Young Turtle walking on tiptoe.

While Turtle was lifting his shell from the bush, Monkey ran to the scarlet flower, and drank the water that lay in its petals.

Then he closed his eyes, and counted slowly:

'Six, seven, eight, nine.'

Turtle tiptoed back to the flower.

'Clever Young Turtle I am,' he chuckled. 'Monkey's still counting. He hasn't seen me. My shell is still safe, so I shan't say the letter.'

Monkey smiled to himself, and waited.

'In I go!' said Clever Young Turtle. 'Back to my bath, with a splash and a splosh.'

A few moments later his angry black eyes stared out over the top of the flower.

'You drank my bath water, Monkey,' he said.

'I'll fill it again from the stream,' said Monkey. 'But not unless you tell me the letter!'

'A!' shouted Turtle. 'Fill up my bath.'

Monkey scooped water into his paws and filled the flower.

Then he danced for joy.

'I know the name of the tree,' he chuckled. 'It's B and A, and N and A, and another N and an A.

BANANA! Jaguar hid my chocolate barrel under the banana tree!'

The sun was getting ready to set when Monkey reached the banana tree. He scratched in the earth with his paws, and said: 'Now I can see the top of my barrel. Now I can see the whole of my barrel. Now I can have my chocolate party.'

He opened the barrel and took out the chocolate.

Along to the party came Monkey's friends: Peccary Pig, and Capybara, the Yellow Frogs, and Jacana Bird, Little Opossum and Armadillo, Anteater, Crabeater Raccoon, Marmoset and Turtle, and Coatimundi, and all the others.

And after that, Crocodile came, and Anaconda, and Pimpla Hog, and the scarlet Thrips, and Pelican, and Clever Young Turtle.

Then along came Jaguar, looking for chocolate. 'Yes, you can come to my party too,' said Monkey.

Everyone sat in a circle, and ate.

They ate the sweet milk chocolate bars; the bars of chocolate filled with toffee, the bars of chocolate scrunchy with nuts, the jelly babies in chocolate cradles, and packets and packets of chocolate peppermint creams.

They left the chocolate mice until last.

'Pull out their string tails,' said Monkey. 'String tails are bad for our tummies.'

'Ha!' said Jaguar. '*I* shan't bother! *I* shan't bother to pull out their tails. I can eat far more if I swallow them whole.'

Jaguar opened his greedy mouth, and swallowed the mice with their string tails.

Then he groaned.

The pain in his tummy was bad.

'I don't like chocolate parties,' he said.

'*We* do,' said Monkey and all his friends.

As the moon rose over the jungle trees, they licked their sticky paws and claws.

'Parties are very nice,' they said.

'Chocolate parties are better still. And this one is quite the best of them all.'

Then they looked at each other, and nodded, and smiled.

Stories of
South-East Asian Animals

illustrated by Margery Gill

A Hat for Rhinoceros

RHINOCEROS found an old straw hat, which he wore on his head to keep off the sun.

It fitted him perfectly.

It kept his head cool.

He did not know what he would do without it.

While he was dozing one day, with his hat on, Monkey came along and stole it. By the time Rhinoceros came to his senses, Monkey was high in a mango tree, with the hat pulled well down over his ears.

Rhinoceros came to the tree and said, 'You'll excuse me mentioning it, but it's *my* hat.'

'Your hat, my hat, whose hat?' said Monkey. 'It's on *my* head, and that's where I'll keep it.'

Rhinoceros did not argue with Monkey. He was much too proud. He said to himself, 'Oh well, I shall just have to manage, I suppose.'

He went to the bank of the great grey river and put himself up to his ears in the mud. But the heat of the sun on his tender bare head was a burning pain. And it made him angry.

He *needed* a hat.

He was *used* to a hat.

He could not do *without* a hat.

He heaved himself out of the mud and said, 'I'll have that hat. I'll have that hat if I have to climb the tree to get it. Disgraceful! That's what it is, disgraceful. A peaceful Rhinoceros finds a hat, and he can't do without it, and *then* what happens? It's stolen, with never a please or thank you. It's time that monkey was taught a lesson, before he starts stealing our tails and our horns.'

Rhinoceros stumped along to the mango tree. Monkey still sat there, with the hat on his head.

Rhinoceros backed away from the tree trunk. He lowered his head and he flicked up his tail.

'Ah-oop one. Ah-oop two. Ah-oop three. And charge!' he said. And he shot at the tree like a great grey rocket. Faster and faster! Bang! He hit it.

The roots of the mango tree shook in the earth, and its branches beat about in the air. Rhinoceros stiffened his legs, and waited. When Monkey fell, he would catch him, and spank him, and then he would make him return the hat.

But the only thing that fell from the tree was a mango fruit, and Rhinoceros ate it, pretending that this was what he had come for.

'But I'll have that hat, I'll have that hat, if I have to fly in the air to get it.'

He went away and found three sticks, which he tied together with strips of grass.

'A three-stick, that's what it is,' he said. 'A long thin three-stick, good for poking.'

He waited till Monkey fell asleep, then he picked up the three-stick and went to the tree. He could see Monkey's tail and the back of the hat.

'Carefully does it,' Rhinoceros said.

He wriggled the three-stick up through the branches and poked at the hat, very gently at first. Then he poked again. Then he pushed. Then he prodded.

'Bother!' he said. 'Is it *stuck* to his head?'

Rhinoceros felt his temper rising. He jabbed and jerked and joggled the three-stick until he was hot and exceedingly angry.

'Off with you, hat. Come off,' he snorted. 'Oh bother, *now* what's happened to it?'

The three-stick had jabbed through the brim of the hat, and Rhinoceros stared at a tiny blue circle where sky could be seen through the little round hole. He dropped the three-stick and said to himself, 'I *will* have that hat.' And he went away.

He wandered far and wide in the jungle, thinking and planning, and wanting his hat. But all his plans seemed silly and useless.

He stopped at last on the edge of the jungle, and there he saw a peculiar sight. Snake, who usually slid in the grass, was lying curled up in a wicker basket.

Sitting in front of the basket, cross-legged, was a small brown man who was playing a pipe.

'I like that music,' Rhinoceros said. 'It's whistly, weavy, sway-about music.'

Out of the basket came Snake's brown head, pointing upwards towards the sky. Then his body came out of the basket too, slowly and smoothly stretching upwards. The small brown man began to move, swaying his body in time to the music. Snake swayed too, bending *his* body; swaying to one side, the other side, back again, swaying and swaying in time to the music.

'Well,' said Rhinoceros. 'What a strange sight! But now I must go. I have plans to make.'

But he did *not* go. He was caught by the music. The tune held him fast and he could not get free of it. Whistling and weaving and slipping about, it seemed to get right inside his head. Then slowly, Rhinoceros started to sway. He felt uncomfortable and giddy, so he tried to stop, but the tune would not let him. Then, just as he thought he would fall on the grass, the brown man took the pipe from his mouth.

The music stopped whistling and Snake stopped swaying. Rhinoceros stood quite still on the grass, but everything seemed to be spinning around him. Snake, the brown man, the sky, and the trees were all mixed up in a whirling dance. By the time he had sorted them out again, the brown man had gone, and Snake was beside him, saying anxiously, 'Are you all right?'

'I think so, thank you,' Rhinoceros said. 'But I felt so giddy I nearly fell over.' Then, seeing that Snake was still looking worried, he tried to smile and make a joke: 'It's lucky I stay on the ground all the time, and don't go climbing trees,' he said. 'If I'd been on a branch, I *should* have gone crash.'

It was then that Rhinoceros thought of Monkey, sitting at home in the mango tree.

And just as quickly, he thought of a plan.

He bent his head, and whispered to Snake.

'Yes,' said Snake, 'I think it would work. But can you whistle, Mr Rhinoceros?'

'Yes,' said Rhinoceros. 'Thrush Bird taught me.'

'Are you sure you remember the tune?' asked Snake.

'I can't forget it,' Rhinoceros said. 'It got itself into my head and it stayed there. To tell you the truth, I'll be glad to get rid of it.'

'Then come,' said Snake, and he glided away. Rhinoceros followed across the jungle until they came to the mango tree.

Monkey still sat there, hat on head.

'I'm afraid there's no basket,' Rhinoceros whispered. 'But perhaps you can lie on that pile of leaves. I'll stand in front of you, here, like this.'

Snake curled up on the pile of leaves, and Rhinoceros whistled the brown man's tune. Whistling and weaving and slipping about, the music went on and on and on. Out of the leaves rose Snake's brown head, pointing upwards towards the sky. His body came out of the leaves as well, slowly and smoothly stretching upwards. Then Snake swayed to one side, the other side, back again, swaying and swaying in time to the music.

Monkey looked down from the mango tree, and he could not take his eyes off Snake, and Rhinoceros went on whistling the tune, and Snake went on swaying and swaying and swaying.

Then, very slowly, Monkey swayed too, bending his body in time to the music. He tried to stop, because he felt giddy. But he could not take his eyes off Snake, and he could not escape from the slippery music. Everything seemed to be spinning around him. Snake,

Rhinoceros, trees and sky were all mixed up in a whirling dance.

It was then that he swayed and swayed and swayed until he swayed right off the mango branch. He crashed through the tree in a shower of leaves and fell on his tail in front of Rhinoceros.

'Well?' said Rhinoceros. 'What do you say?'

'I'm sorry,' said Monkey.

'Good,' said Rhinoceros. 'Now you will kindly return my hat.'

Monkey tugged the hat from his head. Rhinoceros took it and stared at it happily. Then he began to mutter and frown, looking down at the little round hole that the poking three-stick had made in the brim. He had worried about the hole all day. But soon he was smiling again, and saying, 'Of course, of course, how silly I am. I ought to have thought of that before. The hole in the hat is really quite useful.'

He picked a hibiscus flower from a bush, and tucked it carefully into the hole.

He put on the hat and smiled to himself.

'Monkey,' he said. 'Run along and be good. Run along quickly before I spank you.'

Snake looked up at the flower-trimmed hat.

'It fits you perfectly,' he said.

'Yes,' said Rhinoceros. 'Yes, it does. And it keeps my head cool. That's why I wear it.'

He went away to the great grey river, and stood on the bank, very quiet and still.

Was he *really* fast asleep?

The air grew cool and the moon came up, shining

its silver light on the river. And in the shadowy water-mirror, between the rippling reflection of trees, the satisfied face of a big Rhinoceros smiled, beneath a flower-trimmed hat.

The Tree Trick

A MORA tree and a mango tree grew side by side in the jungle. High between the topmost branches a thick creeper rope stretched from tree to tree like a clothes line.

In the mora tree lived the monkey family – Father Monkey, Mother Monkey, and three little smiling monkey children.

Mother and Father sat on the ground, eating juicy mora berries. The three smiling children climbed in the tree, happily playing a circus game. They went to the end of the topmost branch and hung by their hands from the creeper rope. They moved their hands along the rope, swinging across to the mango tree. Then they hid in its branches and no one could see them.

'What are they up to *now*?' said their father. 'They're very quiet all of a sudden.'

'It's only the circus game,' said their mother.

She looked up into the mora tree. No one was there. 'They have gone,' she said. 'They have gone across the creeper rope and they're hiding themselves in the mango tree.'

Father Monkey called: 'Come down. There are juicy mora berries for supper. Come down here, you little monkeys.'

The monkey children came from the mango tree, swinging across the creeper rope to the topmost branch of their own home tree. Then they jumped down the tree from branch to branch and sat in a row to eat their supper.

Along the track bounded great cat Panther, fierce and hungry and hunting for supper. With a thud and a growl he stopped by the tree.

'Ah! My supper at last,' he said. 'Five little fat delicious monkeys!'

The monkey children shook with fright.

'But our skins are tough,' said Father Monkey. 'We're hairy and bony and not nice tasting. Wouldn't you rather eat a goat, or a sheep, or a nice little tender weasel?'

'No,' said Panther. 'I want to eat *you*.'

Father Monkey looked at his children.

'It's really rather strange,' he said. 'The rules must be different, for panthers and monkeys.'

'What rules?' Panther wanted to know.

'The eating rules,' said Father Monkey. 'In the monkey tribe the rule is this: Children eat first, grown-ups after.'

Panther looked at the monkey children.

'Have they eaten their supper yet?' he asked.

Father Monkey said: 'Oh no, they were just going to start when *you* came along.'

'I suppose we must keep to the rules,' said Panther. 'Children eat first, grown-ups after. *They* are children, and I'm a grown-up. They must have their supper before I have mine. Tell them to go and get it, Monkey. But tell them to hurry, and come back quickly.'

Father Monkey looked at the children.

'Go and get your supper,' he said. 'It's up on the topmost branch of the mora tree. Eat it quickly, as Panther tells you.'

He shook his paw at the three little monkeys.

'Don't waste time, do you hear, little monkeys. Don't start playing the circus game.'

But as he spoke he winked an eye.

The little monkeys said, 'Yes, Father, we know *exactly* what you mean.' And up they climbed, until no one could see them.

Panther sat on the ground, waiting.

But the monkey children did not come back.

Panther began to yawn and fidget.

'Why are they taking so long?' he asked.

Father Monkey scratched his head.

'I expect it's because of the rules,' he said.

'What rules?' Panther wanted to know.

'The starting rules,' said Father Monkey. 'In the monkey tribe the rule is this: Children do not eat their supper till Mother Monkey tells them to start.'

'I suppose we must keep to the rules,' said Panther. 'Your children can't start, so how can they finish? Until they have finished, they can't come back. If they don't come back, where is my supper? Tell your wife to climb the tree, so that her monkey children may start.'

Father Monkey smiled and said: 'Monkey wife, go up the tree. Tell the children to eat their supper. Then bring them back quickly, for Panther is hungry.'

But as he spoke he winked an eye.

Mother Monkey said: 'My dear, I understand *perfectly* what you mean.' She climbed and climbed until no one could see her.

Panther sat on the ground, waiting.

But Mother Monkey did not come back. Nor did the little monkey children. Panther began to sigh and shuffle.

'Why is she taking so long?' he asked.

Father Monkey waved a paw.

'I expect it's because of the rules,' he said.

'What rules?' Panther wanted to know.

'The coming down rules,' said Father Monkey. 'In

the monkey tribe the rule is this: Mother follows
Father's tail.'

Panther growled in his throat and said, 'I am growing tired of these rules, rules, rules. Climb up the
tree, and then come back, and tell your wife to follow
your tail. And don't forget to bring the children.'

'Just as you say,' said Father Monkey. And away
he went, climbing fast.

Panther waited, yawning and fidgeting.

He waited still longer, sighing and shuffling.

'Why are you taking so long?' he shouted. 'Come
down here, or I'll climb up and fetch you.'

There was no answer.

Panther started to climb through the branches, but he could not see the five fat monkeys. He *did* see the creeper rope stretching out, joined to the mango tree, like a clothes line.

'I mustn't step on *that*,' he said. 'It's much too thin for a panther's weight.'

He stood at last on the topmost branch, but not a tail or a paw could he see. And then he was quite the most puzzled panther that ever lost a monkey family.

'Where can they be?' he said to himself. 'They are certainly not in this mora tree. And they didn't come down, so they must have gone up.'

He stared up into the empty sky.

'How did they do it?' he said to himself. 'How did

they climb up and up to the top, and suddenly vanish to nothing at all?'

Panther climbed down, sadly and slowly, because he was trying to think of an answer. He went far away, without any supper, and thought all that evening, and all the next day, and the day after that. But his thinking was useless. None of his answers was right, and he knew it.

The only right answer was back in the jungle, where the mora and mango trees grew, side by side. From the topmost branch of the mango tree came Father Monkey, Mother Monkey, and three little smiling monkey children. They went one by one to the end of the branch, and hung from the creeper rope by their hands. They moved their hands along the rope, swinging across to the mora tree.

'It's good to be back again,' they said. 'It's good to be back in our own home tree.'

Then they smiled at each other, and ate their supper.

Upside-down Loris

HIGH on a tree lay small furry Loris, flat on his tummy along a branch.

Far below, on the jungle track, big and little creatures passed. Loris stared down from his tree top to watch them.

Elephant passed, going to his mud bath.

'He's strong,' said Loris. 'I wish I were strong.'

Panther passed, going to his hunting.

'He's brave,' said Loris. 'I wish I were brave.'

Fox passed, going to his burrow.

'He's clever,' said Loris. 'I wish I were clever.'

He crept through the tree, hiding his eyes, as though he were very ashamed of himself. Then he snatched at a Christmas fly, and caught it. He hung upside-down, high in the tree, with his strong little feet gripping the branch and the Christmas fly between his hands. He put the fly in his mouth and crunched it.

'I don't like being a Loris,' he said, as he swung upside-down in the top of the tree. 'I wish I were strong and brave and clever, instead of being so fat and slow.'

He crept to his tree hole and curled himself up, but his big round shining eyes were open. He felt too miserable to sleep.

From the track below came a loud, gruff voice, the voice of Rhinoceros saying, 'No. I don't believe it. No indeed. I tell you I simply don't believe it.'

'I wonder *what* he doesn't believe,' said Loris, peeping out of his hole.

Rhinoceros raised his great grey head and stared at fat little furry Loris. 'Ah!' he rumbled. 'A tree-living creature! In that case you'll probably know the others. Is this the right track for the cat bear's tree? If not, could you kindly show me the way?'

Loris crept from branch to branch, slowly coming down the tree. Rhinoceros waited patiently, a kindly smile on his horny face.

'I'm sorry to give you the trouble,' he said. 'But I'm anxious to see the baby cat bear. They say she can hang upside-down in a tree, and I don't believe it. No indeed. I tell you I simply don't believe it.'

Loris lifted his small furry head and looked at huge Rhinoceros.

'Do *you* want to hang in a tree?' he asked.

Rhinoceros blinked his little black eyes and his wrinkled face was sad as he said, 'I don't want to *do* it, I just want to see it.'

Tiny Loris and great Rhinoceros walked together across the jungle, Rhinoceros heavy on leathery legs, and Loris shuffling sadly beside him. At last they reached the cat bear's tree, and high on a branch they saw a creature, a small, shaggy creature, upside-down, hanging by her tiny tail. Rhinoceros opened his big pink mouth and smiled at the little baby cat bear. Cat Bear saw his jagged teeth. She squeaked with fright, and fell off the branch.

'There!' said Rhinoceros. 'Just as I thought. Cat bear's *can't* hang upside-down.'

Loris said shyly, 'Bat can do it. Bat hangs upside-down when he sleeps.'

'I don't believe it,' Rhinoceros said. 'I tell you I simply don't believe it. But nevertheless I *want* to believe it. So let's go and look. Lead the way, little creature.'

Bat was asleep near the mouth of his cave, hanging upside-down from a branch with his black wings folded about his head.

Rhinoceros smiled all over his face, and sighed a contented, rumbling sigh.

Bat looked down. 'That's thunder,' he said. 'The

gnats will be flying, and I must fly too.' He dropped from the branch and whirled away.

Rhinoceros said, 'You see. He can't hang.' And he looked so unhappy that Loris felt sorry.

'Nuthatch Bird can do it,' he whispered. 'He can hang upside-down from a twig.'

They went to the cotton tree, side by side, Rhinoceros muttering, 'No, not true. I tell you I simply don't believe it.' They stood by the cotton tree, staring upwards. High above them was Nuthatch Bird, hanging upside-down from a twig, and jabbing his beak in a flower, for insects.

Rhinoceros smiled. Then out of the flower danced a tiny white moth, and Nuthatch Bird chased it. Rhinoceros did not say a word. He stared at the ground, and his tail hung limply.

Then Loris forgot how small he was. He forgot how enormous Rhinoceros was. He crept up close to the huge horny creature and gently patted his knobbly grey knee.

'Thank you,' said Rhinoceros. 'Thank you for being so patient and kind with a silly great creature who ought to know better.'

His little black eyes stared sadly at Loris.

'Do you mind if I tell you about it?' he said. 'I've never told anyone this before, but you seem to be so understanding. You see, I am strong, and they say I am brave, and sometimes they even say I am clever. But when I heard of the upside-down creatures, I knew that of all the things in the jungle, the strongest, bravest, cleverest thing is to hang upside-down in a tree.'

Rhinoceros stared at his feet, and went on, 'I know that I can never do it, but I did want to see it, just once.'

Loris looked at the tree above them. He looked at the sorrowful face of Rhinoceros. And he knew that the time had come to forget that his own little body was fat and slow.

He blinked his eyes and whispered shyly, 'I can do it, Mr Rhinoceros. I can hang upside-down in a tree.'

Slowly he climbed up on to a branch. He snatched at a Christmas fly and caught it. Then he hung upside-down, high in the tree, with his strong little feet gripping the branch, and the Christmas fly between his hands. He put the fly in his mouth and crunched it.

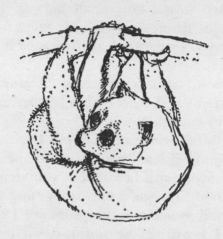

Rhinoceros stared. He believed it. At last!

He sighed a rumbling, contented sigh.

'How strong!' he said. 'Oh, well done, little creature. How strong. Oh, how brave. Oh, how clever you are!'

Loris came down to the ground, slowly, but now his eyes were shining with happiness. And as soon as he saw the look of delight and the big smile of joy on the face of Rhinoceros, Loris knew that never again would he want to be anyone else but himself.

Rhinoceros said he was strong.

Rhinoceros said he was brave.

Rhinoceros even said he was clever.

Proudly he lifted his small furry head, smiling up at his great grey friend. Then tiny Loris and great Rhinoceros walked together across the jungle, back to Loris's own home tree. They walked together, and talked together, and smiled at each other, as good friends will.

The Stamping Elephant

ELEPHANT stamped about in the jungle, thumping down his great grey feet on the grass and the flowers and the small soft animals.

He squashed the tiny shiny creatures and trod on the tails of the creeping creatures. He beat down the

232

corn seedlings, crushed the lilacs, and stamped on the morning glory flowers.

'We must stop all this stamping,' said Goat, Snake, and Mouse.

Goat said, 'Yes, we must stop it. But *you* can't do anything, Mouse.'

And Snake said, 'Of course she can't. Oh no, *you* can't do anything, Mouse.'

Mouse said nothing. She sat on the grass and listened while Goat told his plan.

'Scare him, that's what I'll do,' said Goat. 'Oh good good good, I'll scare old Elephant, frighten him out of his wits I will.'

He found an empty turtle shell and hung it up on a low branch. Then he beat on the shell with his horns.

'This is my elephant-scaring drum. I shall beat it, clatter clatter,' he said. 'Elephant will run away. Oh, good good good.'

Stamp stamp stamp. Along came Elephant.

Goat tossed his head and ran at the shell, clatter, clatter, beating it with his horns.

'Oh, what a clatter I'm making,' he bleated. 'Oh, what a terrible, elephant-scaring, horrible clatter.'

Elephant said, '*What* a nasty little noise!'

He took the shell in his long trunk, lifted it high up into the air, and banged it down on Goat's hairy head. Then he went on his way, stamping.

Mouse said nothing. But she thought, 'Poor old Goat looks sad, standing there with a shell on his head.' Then she sat on the grass and listened while Snake told his plan.

'I shall make myself into a rope,' said Snake. 'Yes yes yes, that's what I'll do.' He looped his body around a tree trunk. 'Now I'm an elephant-catching rope. Yes yes yes, that's what I am. I shall hold old Elephant tight by the leg, and I shan't let him go. No, I shan't let him go, till he promises not to stamp any more.'

Stamp stamp stamp. Along came Elephant.

Snake hid in the long grass. Elephant stopped beside a tree, propped up his two white tusks on a branch, and settled himself for a nice little sleep.

Snake came sliding out of the grass. He looped his long body around the tree trunk and around old Elephant's leg as well. His teeth met his tail at the end of the loop, and he bit on his tail tip, holding fast.

'I have looped old Elephant's leg to the tree trunk. Now I must hold on tight,' he thought.

Elephant woke, and tried to move. But with only three legs he was helpless.

'Why are you holding my leg?' he shouted.

Snake kept quiet. He could not speak. If he opened his mouth the loop would break.

Elephant put his trunk to the ground and filled it with tickling yellow dust. Then he snorted, and blew the dust at Snake.

Snake wriggled. He wanted to sneeze.

Elephant put his trunk to the ground and sniffed up more of the tickling dust. 'Poof!' he said, and he blew it at Snake.

Snake held his breath and wriggled and squirmed, trying his hardest not to sneeze. But the dust was too tickly. 'Ah ah ah!' He closed his eyes and opened his mouth. 'Ah ah tishoo!' The loop was broken.

Elephant said, '*What* a nasty little cold!'

And he went on his way, stamping.

Mouse said nothing. But she thought, 'Snake looks sad, lying there sneezing his head off.' Then she sat on the grass and made her own plan.

Stamp stamp stamp. Along came Elephant. Mouse peeped out of her hole and watched him. He lay on his side, stretched out his legs, and settled himself for a nice long sleep.

Mouse breathed deeply, and stiffened her whiskers. She waited till Elephant closed his eyes. Then she crept through the grass like a little grey shadow, her bright brown eyes watching Elephant's trunk. She made her way slowly around his great feet, and tip-toed past his shining tusks. She trotted along by his leathery trunk until she was close to its tender pink tip. Then suddenly, skip! she darted backwards, and sat in the end of Elephant's trunk.

Elephant opened his eyes, and said: 'Can't I have *any* peace in this jungle? First it's a silly clattering goat, then it's a sillier sneezing snake, and now it's a mouse, the smallest of all, and quite the silliest. That's what *I* think.'

He looked down his long grey trunk and said, 'Oh yes, I know you are there, little mouse, because I can see your nose and whiskers. Out you get! Do you hear, little mouse?'

'Eek,' said Mouse, 'I won't get out, unless you promise not to stamp.'

'Then I'll shake you out,' Elephant shouted, and he swung his trunk from side to side.

'Thank you,' squeaked Mouse. 'I'm having a ride. It's almost like flying. Thank you, Elephant.'

Elephant shouted, 'I'll drown you out.' He stamped to the river and waded in, dipping the end of his trunk in the water.

'Thank you,' squeaked Mouse. 'I'm having a swim. It's almost like diving. Thank you, Elephant.'

Elephant stood on the bank, thinking. He could not pull down leaves for his dinner. He could not give himself a bath. He could not live, with a mouse in his trunk:

'Please, little mouse, get out of my trunk. Please,' he said.

'Will you promise not to stamp?' asked Mouse.

'No,' said Elephant.

'Then this is what I shall do,' said Mouse, and she tickled his trunk with her tail.

'Now will you promise not to stamp?'

'No,' said Elephant.

'Then this is what I shall do,' said Mouse and she nipped his trunk with her sharp little teeth.

'Yes,' squealed Elephant. 'Yes yes yes.'

Mouse ran back to her hole, and waited.

Step step step. Along came Elephant, walking

gently on great grey feet. He saw the tiny shiny creatures, and waited until they scuttled away. He saw the little creeping creatures, and stepped very carefully over their tails.

'Elephant doesn't stamp any more. *Someone* has stopped him,' the creatures said. 'Someone big and brave and clever.'

Goat said: 'I think Mouse did it.'

And Snake said: 'Oh yes, that is right. Mouse did it.'

And not far away, at the foot of a tree, a small, contented, tired little mouse sat on the grass and smiled to herself.

Who Stole the Supper Frogs?

MONGOOSE lived in a long black tunnel, underneath a juniper tree.

'It's supper time. Supper time. Good!' he said, trotting happily up the tunnel. 'Now what shall I have? I'm very very hungry. Four little frogs would be nice, I think. I'll run through the cane beds and catch them by the river.'

Off he went to the deep brown river, running through the cane beds and singing to himself:

'Four little supper frogs, I'll catch them very soon.
The first will be as yellow as the big round jungle
    moon.'

The little yellow supper frog was sitting on the bank. Mongoose caught it and carried it home. He pushed it into the tunnel and said, 'In you go, frog that is yellow as the moon. That's the first for my supper.' And he turned his back and ran through the cane beds.

The little yellow supper frog waited for a minute. Then he hopped from the tunnel, and under the tree, and away through the jungle grass.

He would not be eaten.

Mongoose did not see him go. He went on his way to the river, singing:

'Four little supper frogs, playing "up and under".
The second will be grey as clouds that come before
    the thunder.'

The little grey supper frog was splashing in the water, playing a game of 'up and under'. Mongoose caught it and carried it home. He pushed it into the tunnel and said, 'In you go, frog that is grey as the clouds. That's the second for my supper.' And he turned his back and ran through the cane beds.

The little grey supper frog waited for a minute.
Then he hopped from the tunnel, and under the tree,
and away through the pine trees.

He was no one's supper.

Mongoose did not see him go. He went on his way
to the river, singing:

'Four little supper frogs singing in the rain.
The third will be as green as grass that grows upon
the plain.'

The little green supper frog was singing to itself.
Mongoose caught it and carried it home. He pushed it
into the tunnel and said, 'In you go, frog that is green
as the grass. That's the third for my supper.' And he
turned his back and ran through the cane beds.

The little green supper frog waited for a minute.
Then he hopped from the tunnel, and under the tree,
and away through the laurels.

Get eaten? Not he!

Mongoose did not see him go. He went on his way to
the river, singing:

'Four little supper frogs hopping in the mud.
The fourth is red as mowha flowers come freshly
from the bud.'

The little red supper frog was hopping in a puddle.
Mongoose caught it and carried it home. He pushed
it into the tunnel and said, 'In you go, frog that is
red as a flower. That's the fourth for my supper.

'Four little supper frogs, fat little friskers.
And now, before I eat them up, I'll wash my paws
and whiskers.'

And off he went, running through the cane
beds.

Out of the tunnel, and under the tree, and away
through the ferns hopped the little red frog. Mongoose did not see him go. He dipped his paws in the
river water and rubbed them over his dusty whiskers.
Then he went home.

'In I go, Mongoose as thin as a rope,' he said. And
his tail disappeared in the long dark tunnel.

Then out of the tunnel came peculiar noises;
gruntings and grumblings and scamperings and
scratchings.

And out of the tunnel came Mongoose.

He sat beneath the juniper tree, with his tail on
the ground and his nose in the air, and he moaned and
groaned and grizzled and grumbled, and at last he
raised his voice and called, 'Who stole my supper
frogs? Who stole my supper frogs?'

Over the grass came a heavy, hairy creature, with
thick black legs and a wide grey back.

'Tell me,' said Mongoose. 'Did *you* steal the supper
frogs?'

'No,' said Honey Badger. 'Nasty little salty things.
I had honey. It's sweeter than frogs.'

Then Mongoose and Honey Badger sat together,
underneath the juniper tree, calling, 'Who stole the
supper frogs? Who stole the supper frogs?'

Between the pines came a soft, furry creature, with whiskers, and gleaming yellow eyes.

'Fishing Cat,' said Mongoose. 'Did *you* steal the supper frogs?'

'No,' said Fishing Cat. 'Horrible dull things. *I* had fish. It's tastier than frogs.'

Then Mongoose, Badger, and Fishing Cat sat side by side, underneath the tree, calling, 'Who stole the supper frogs?'

Between the laurels came a hairy little creature, with tiny black eyes and sticking-out teeth.

'Rat,' said Mongoose. 'Did *you* steal the supper frogs?'

'No,' said Rat. 'They're much too jumpy. *I* had roots. They're easier to catch.'

Then Mongoose, Badger, Fishing Cat and Rat called, 'Who stole the supper frogs? Who stole the supper frogs?'

Between the ferns came a sleek, quick creature, with a long brown body and a pointed face.

'Weasel,' said Mongoose. 'Did *you* steal the supper frogs?'

'No,' said Weasel. 'Their skins are thick and lumpy. *I* had birds' eggs. They're easier to eat.'

Mongoose, Badger, Cat, Rat, and Weasel sat beneath the juniper tree. They raised their voices and called, 'Who stole them? *Somebody* stole them. Who stole the supper frogs?'

Then Mongoose, Badger, Cat, Rat, and Weasel went to the river to look for the frogs. They sat on the bank and stared at the water, and when they heard four little splashes they said, 'Oh listen! Four little fish in the water.'

They did not see the supper frogs.

'Somebody stole them. Who was it?' they called. 'Who stole the supper frogs? Let's ask Lion.'

'Yes, we will go and ask Lion,' said Mongoose. 'Which is the way to his den? Which way?'

There were four little splashes, and four little frogs sat on the other side of the river.

'North,' said the yellow frog.

'South,' said the grey frog.

'East,' said the green frog.

'West,' said the red frog.

And each of them pointed in a different direction.

Mongoose, Badger, Cat, Rat, and Weasel looked around in the different directions. And while they were staring round about them, there were four little splashes, and four little frogs jumped in the water and swam away.

Mongoose, Badger, Cat, Rat, and Weasel stared along the river, and said, 'There they go. There go the supper frogs. *Nobody* stole them. They swam away.'

Mongoose said in a quiet sad voice, 'They swam away and left me hungry.'

Off went Badger, Cat, Rat, and Weasel. Mongoose sat on the river bank, wondering why such miserable things should happen to a lonely, unhappy little Mongoose. He had found his supper, and lost it again. He had found some friends, and lost them too.

With his tail on the ground and his nose in the air,

he stared at nothing, trying not to cry. He was all alone, and nobody came. He was dreadfully hungry, and nobody cared.

Then back came Badger, carrying honey. Back came Fishing Cat, carrying fish. Back came Rat, carrying roots. Back came Weasel, carrying birds' eggs. 'We thought you would like some supper,' they said.

Mongoose sat on the river bank, smiling and happy with his four good friends, wondering why he bothered with frogs when honey and fish and roots and eggs could taste so delicious for his supper.

Terrible Tiger's Party

'A TEA party, that's what I'll have,' said Tiger. 'Not
an A party, or a B party, or a C party, but a T party.
So all the things at my party must be T things, like
tart, and toffee, and tapioca.'

Terrible Tiger went to a teak tree. He sat on the ground. His great voice roared, 'Come to my T party. Come to the teak tree, Tree-mouse, Toddy Cat, and Two-horned Rhinoceros. Come to my T party.'

They came to the party but they forgot to bring a present.

Tiger lifted his great yellow head and his rough voice roared out over the jungle, 'Where is my present, my T party present? Where is my T present?'

Tree-mouse, Toddy Cat and Two-horned Rhinoceros stood in a row and looked at their feet. Then they said, 'We forgot it. We're dreadfully sorry. Would a turtle-top suit you, or a tree-pie bird, or perhaps a tin of treacle for a very special treat?'

'No,' roared Tiger. 'Bring me a tiger lily.'

Mouse said, 'I beg your pardon, Mr Tiger, but there is no such thing. There is not a mouse lily.'

Cat said, 'There is not a cat lily.'

Rhinoceros said, 'There is not a rhinoceros lily. So why should there be a tiger lily?'

'Because I say there *is*,' roared Tiger. 'Get me a tiger lily. Get it, I tell you.'

Tree-mouse, Toddy Cat, and Two-horned Rhinoceros searched in the swamp and they searched in the rice fields. But they could not find a tiger lily.

'I'm tired,' said Tree-mouse. 'Take him a turtle-top.'

So back they went to the teak tree, and said: 'We're sorry, Mr Tiger, we couldn't find the tiger

248

lily. We've brought you back a turtle-top to shade you from the sun.'

Terrible Tiger swished his tail.

'It isn't a turtle-top at all,' he growled. 'It's a shell, I tell you. Get me a tiger lily.'

Tree-mouse, Toddy Cat, and Two-horned Rhinoceros searched among the mango trees and they searched among the sheeshum trees. But they could not find the tiger lily.

'What's the use of trying any longer?' said Toddy Cat. 'Take old Tiger a tree-pie bird.'

So back they went to the teak tree and said, 'We're sorry, Mr Tiger, the lily wasn't there. So we've brought you back a tree-pie to sing you a song.'

Terrible Tiger showed his teeth.

'It isn't a tree-pie at all,' he growled. 'It's a bird I tell you. Get me a tiger lily.'

Tree-mouse, Toddy Cat, and Two-horned Rhinoceros looked beneath the magnolia flowers and they looked beneath the rhododendrons, but they could not find the tiger lily.

'It's just a lot of trouble for nothing,' said Rhinoceros. 'Take old Tiger some honey from the bees. I know he likes it. I've seen him eating it, and licking his lips, and smiling to himself.'

'Honey's not a T thing,' Toddy Cat said. 'Terrible Tiger is having a T party. Honey is a H thing. It won't do at all.'

'Bother old Terrible Tiger,' said Rhinoceros.

'We'll tell him it's treacle. He'll never know the difference.'

They found a tin and filled it with honey. Then back to the teak tree they went and said, 'We're sorry, Mr Tiger, we couldn't find the lily, so we've brought you back some treacle for a very special treat.'

Terrible Tiger lost his temper. He snarled and he roared and he gnashed his teeth. Tree-mouse, Toddy Cat, and Two-horned Rhinoceros said, 'What a fuss!' and they ran away to hide. They sat on the grass behind a rhododendron bush.

Tiger thought they had gone for ever.

He stopped roaring, and smiled to himself.

He took one tiny taste of the honey.

'It's delicious,' he said. 'I like it. I shall eat it.'

He pushed his bristly face in the tin, and licked

and licked till his ears and nose and whiskers were sticky all over with the sweet, yellow honey.

And because his face was in the tin, he did not see the stinging bees that came buzzing into the teak tree branches.

Buzz came the first bee.

Buzz came the second bee.

Buzz buzz buzz came a hundred busy stinging bees.

When Tiger had emptied the honey tin he yawned. 'Delicious!' he said. 'And now I'll go to sleep.'

The bees looked down at the sweet yellow honey that was sticking to his ears and his nose and his whiskers.

Buzz came the first bee.

Buzz came the second bee.

Buzz buzz buzz came a hundred busy stinging bees.

They sat on Terrible Tiger's head, and licked at the honey on his bristly face.

Terrible Tiger swished his tail. He snarled and he roared and he lost his temper. He banged at the bees with his paw, and shouted, 'Stop it! I'm Terrible Tiger, I tell you. Stop it! Stop it at once, I tell you.'

The bees were exceedingly cross with Tiger. They stung him on his ears and his bristly face. Terrible Tiger sprang in the air. He ran through the jungle roaring with rage, and the stinging bees chased him, buzzing round his head.

Tree-mouse, Toddy Cat, and Two-horned Rhinoceros came from behind the bush to watch.

'Look,' they said. 'Look at the bees. Terrible Tiger was tired of his T party, even before he really began it. He's found something better. Look at the bees. Terrible Tiger is having a B party.'

They watched until Tiger had disappeared. Then they went to the teak tree and sat down beneath it. The turtle-top shaded their eyes from the sun, and the tree-pie bird sat on a branch, and sang.

'Now we can have our party,' they said. 'But we can't have a T party. Where are the T things?'

Tree-mouse said, '*I* shall eat buds.'

Toddy Cat said, '*I* shall eat fruit.'

Rhinoceros said, '*I* shall eat grass.'

'Good!' they said. 'We're having an I party. Poor old Tiger. Perhaps he'd like to come.'

But where was Tiger? No one knew.

'I don't know. I don't know. I don't know,' they said together.

And where was the tiger lily?

I don't know.

The Apricot Race

THE sweet yellow apricot lay on the ground, ready for eating.

Rhinoceros saw it.

Brown Bear saw it.

Civet Cat saw it.

And they all said, '*I* want it.'

Then they stood in a row looking down at the apricot; big Rhinoceros, fat and horny; big Brown

Bear, fierce and shaggy; long low Civet, sleek and small.

Rhinoceros said, 'The apricot goes to the best thumper. Not to the one who jumps the highest, but the one who comes down with the loudest thump. The apricot goes to *him*.'

'No,' said Brown Bear. 'The apricot goes to the best growler. Not to the one who makes the most noise, but the one who growls the terrible growl that makes you shiver and hide your head. The apricot goes to *him*.'

'No,' said Civet. 'The apricot goes to the longest tail. Not to the one with the fluffiest tail, or the bushiest tail, or the swishiest tail, but the one with the sleekest, longest tail. The apricot goes to *him*.'

'We agree,' said Rhinoceros, Bear, and Civet. 'The apricot goes to the best thumper, the fiercest growler, the longest tail. That is quite right. But who will judge?'

Whoop-whoop-whoop came little black Monkey, leaping lightly from tree to tree. And he swung between the jungle branches until he was over the very spot where Rhinoceros, Bear, and Civet stood. They looked up into the branches and said, 'Stop, you black little leaping creature with wise white whiskers around your face. Come down here. *You* shall judge.'

Monkey came down and walked on the ground, with his tail curled up like a question mark. He looked at Rhinoceros, Bear, and Civet. And he looked at the apricot.

'It's not for you,' Rhinoceros said. 'It goes to the one who can thump the loudest. Civet is smallest, so he can thump first. Listen, Monkey, and say who is best.'

Civet jumped as high as a bush, but when he came down there was no thump at all.

Brown Bear jumped as high as a fern, but the thump that he made when he came to the ground could only be heard three trees away.

Then Rhinoceros closed his eyes, and snorted, and lifted all four legs off the ground. He only jumped as high as a grass stalk, but when he came down to the earth again, the thump that he made was a thunderous thump, so that all the birds for miles around came swooping and chirruping out of the trees.

Then the three of them stood in a row, and said, 'Tell us, Monkey. Who was best?'

Monkey looked at the yellow apricot, thinking how sweet it would taste in his mouth. He did not want it to go to Rhinoceros.

'I'm sorry. I can't decide,' he said. 'I don't know which of you thumped the loudest.'

'Then we'll growl,' said Bear. 'Rhinoceros first. Listen, Monkey, and then you must judge.'

Rhinoceros frowned, and tried to growl. But out of his wide pink mouth came a snuffle, as though he were trying to sneeze, or purr.

Civet tried next, but he only mewed, as though he wanted someone to stroke him.

Then Brown Bear's ears came slanting forward, and the growl that he made was a terrible growl, so

that all the creatures for miles around hid their heads and shivered with fright.

Rhinoceros shivered, and hid *his* head.

Civet shivered, and hid his head.

But Monkey kept his eyes wide open, and stretched out his paw to the apricot.

'Tell us,' said Bear, so that Monkey jumped, and put his paws behind his back. 'Tell us, Monkey. Who was best?'

Monkey looked at the apricot. He did not want it to go to Bear.

'I'm sorry. I can't decide,' he told them. 'I don't know which was the fiercest growl.'

'Then it's tails,' said Civet. 'Tell us, Monkey. Who has the sleekest, longest tail?'

Rhinoceros, Bear, and Civet turned round, and stood in a row in front of Monkey, their tails towards him.

Monkey looked. The tail that hung on the end of Rhinoceros did not seem to suit him at all. It dangled straight down like a piece of grey string, with a shaggy tassel right on the end.

The tail on Bear was stumpy and blunt. It hardly seemed to be there at all.

But Civet's tail was ringed, gold and grey, a long, sleek, beautiful tail.

Monkey looked at the three tails, and his paw stretched out slowly to touch the apricot.

'Well?' said Civet, turning around, so that Monkey squeaked, and sat on his paws. 'Well? Whose tail is the longest, Monkey?'

Monkey looked at the apricot. He did not want it to go to Civet.

'I'm sorry. I can't decide,' he told them. 'I don't know which is the longest tail.'

'Then who has the apricot?' Brown Bear asked. 'Who is to eat it? Tell us, Monkey.'

Monkey pointed across the plain to a mango tree, far away on a hill.

'Race to the mango tree and back. The apricot goes to the fastest runner.'

They stood in a row, ready to run.

Monkey called, 'Paws ready. Tails steady. Go!'

Then he sat very still, for a very long time, watching Rhinoceros, Bear and Civet until they were three black specks far away.

Then he stretched out his paw, and touched the apricot.

When the creatures raced away they left three things behind them.

There was the tree.

Beneath the tree, there was Monkey.

In front of Monkey, there was the apricot.

When they came back again, the three things were rather different.

There was the tree.

Beneath the tree, there was a flat patch of grass where Monkey had been sitting.

In front of the place where Monkey had been sitting, there was a dry, dusty apricot stone, and a little bit of yellow skin.

The Challenging Bull

BULL came trotting over the plain, very, very pleased with himself.

He was fat, because he was too lazy to use his strength. He was foolish, because he was too lazy to use his brain.

But just the same, he was very, very pleased with himself.

At the edge of the plain Bull met Elephant. He kicked his heels in the dust, and shouted:

'I am the Challenging Bull of the plain,
The Bull of great strength and remarkable brain.
On land which is dry and on sea which is wetter,
Anything you can do I can do better.
I challenge you.'

Elephant said, 'What is your challenge?'

'I challenge you to stand on your head,' said Bull.

Elephant knelt on his big front knees, with his back legs stiff and his tail in the air. He rested the top of his head on the ground and waggled and jiggled until he was tired.

Bull began to bellow with laughter. He laughed until he lost his breath.

Elephant stood up straight and said, 'Show me how *you* stand on *your* head, Bull.'

Bull said, 'Oh well, yesterday I could have shown you. Tomorrow, perhaps, I could show you. But to-day I lay in the sun too long, and it just so happens my head is aching. How can I stand on my head, when it aches?'

And he tossed his horns and trotted away.

At the edge of the jungle Bull met Goat. He flicked his tail in the air, and shouted:

'I am the Challenging Bull of the plain,
The Bull of great strength and remarkable brain.
On land which is dry and on sea which is wetter,
Anything you can do I can do better.
I challenge you.'

Goat said, 'What is your challenge?'

'I challenge you to climb up that creeper rope,' said Bull.

Goat went and stood by the creeper rope, which was hanging down from a high branch. He jumped at it, held it, and snap! It broke. He sat on his tail with a thump that hurt, and the creeper rope fell on his frightened head and tangled itself around his horns.

Bull began to bellow with laughter. He laughed until it made him ache.

Goat tossed the creeper rope out of his horns.

'Show me how *you* climb a creeper,' he said.

Bull said, 'Oh well, yesterday I could have shown you. Tomorrow, perhaps, I could show you. But to-day I walked on the river sand, and it just so happens my hooves are slippery. How can I hold with my hooves, when they slip?'

And he tossed his horns and trotted away.

At the edge of the swamp Bull met Rhinoceros. He lifted his head to the sky, and shouted:

'I am the Challenging Bull of the plain,
The Bull of great strength and remarkable brain.
On land which is dry and on sea which is wetter,
Anything you can do I can do better.
I challenge you.'

Rhinoceros said, 'What is your challenge?'
'I challenge you to hop on three legs,' said Bull.
Rhinoceros stood by the side of the swamp, shaking each of his legs in turn, to find out which were the strongest three. Then he bent his left front leg beneath him, and made a hop that changed to a wobble. The wobble got worse and Rhinoceros toppled, and fell with a splash in the muddy swamp.

Bull began to bellow with laughter. He laughed until it hurt his ribs.

Rhinoceros rose from the swamp, and said, 'Show me how *you* hop on *your* three legs.'

Bull said, 'Oh well, yesterday I could have shown you. Tomorrow, perhaps, I could show you. But today I ran in the prickly grass and it just so happens it made my legs hurt. How can I hop on three legs, when they hurt?'

And he tossed his horns and trotted away.

He went to the top of a hill, but he did not see *anyone*. There was no one to challenge.

'They have all run away from great Bull,' he snorted. 'They're afraid that great Bull of the plain will challenge them. Ha! They're afraid! They're afraid of great Bull.'

Out of a hole popped little Red Rat.

'You can challenge *me*, if you like,' he said.

Bull's silly laughter was louder than ever.

'You, who are only as big as my ear! *You* couldn't stand on your head,' he shouted.

'It just so happens I can,' said Rat. And he stood on his head, kicking his legs, and smiling all over his upside-down face.

'Oh well,' said Bull. 'It's easy enough if your head doesn't ache. But you couldn't climb a creeper rope.'

'It just so happens I can,' said Rat. And he ran to a creeper that hung from a branch, and climbed to the top, flicking his tail.

'Oh well,' said Bull. 'It's easy enough if your paws don't slip. But you couldn't hop on three legs.'

'It just so happens I can,' said Rat. And he bent his right front leg beneath him, and bounced up and down like a red rubber ball.

'Oh well,' said Bull. 'It's easy enough if your legs don't hurt, but you couldn't ... you couldn't ...'

'What?' said Rat.

Bull was not laughing any more as he stood on top of the hill with Rat. Bull's little brain was trying to think.

He looked down the hill and saw a tree. It was tall as a tower and firm as a rock. Its trunk was knobbled and thick with age, and its branches reached out like the arms of a giant.

Then Bull looked down at little Red Rat, who was sitting beside a tuft of grass.

'You couldn't knock down that tree,' he said.

Little Red Rat sighed deeply, and said, 'It's a very big job for a very small rat. But *you* are a big Bull. Why don't *you* try?'

Bull's little brain could not find an excuse, so he braced his legs on the ground and said:

'I'll charge at it fiercely and hit with my head.
I'll smite it and smash it and knock it down dead.'

266

With a thunder of hooves and a kicking of dust he charged down the hillside and ran at the tree trunk, banging it crash! with his head.

The tree did not even shiver.

Bull came back to the top of the hill.

He said, 'Of course, that was only the first hit, to loosen the roots.'

With a tossing of horns and flicking of tail he ran down the hill again straight at the tree trunk. Crash! He hit it with his head.

A little dead twig came falling down.

Bull limped wearily up the hill.

He said, 'Of course, that's only the second hit, to weaken the trunk.'

He made a wobbly run down the hillside. Bang! His head crashed into the trunk.

A leaf floated gently down to the ground.

Bull staggered back to the top of the hill, and he panted for breath as he said, 'That's the third hit, the third hit. Oh dear, it's the last hit. Oh dear, I feel dreadful. I really feel dreadful.'

And then he fell down on the grass with his eyes closed.

Rat went quietly down the hillside.

Nibble nibble nibble. His teeth went nibble nibble nibble at the tree trunk.

Elephant, Goat, and Rhinoceros came. They sat on the top of the hill to watch.

And the Challenging Bull lay fast asleep, dreaming beneath the midday sun.

Nibble nibble nibble. Nibble nibble nibble.

Minute after minute, and hour after hour, as the sun moved slowly across the sky, Rat's little teeth were eating through the tree trunk.

Nibble nibble nibble. The tree sighed, and rustled its leaves.

And the Challenging Bull lay fast asleep as the sun sank low and the shadows lengthened.

Nibble nibble nibble.

The tree groaned, and shuffled its branches.

Nibble nibble nibble.

The tree moaned, and swayed on its trunk. It held its branches up to the sky. But it could not stand. It was hurt and helpless. It tilted slowly towards the hill.

Rat disappeared.

Elephant, Goat, and Rhinoceros ran back out of danger.

But the Challenging Bull stayed just where he was, fast asleep in the darkening shadows.

For a minute the tree seemed to hang in the air, holding itself above the hillside.

Then it fell. Splintering, snapping, cracking and swishing, it threw itself heavily on to the ground.

Nobody spoke. Nobody moved. It seemed as though they were waiting for something.

Then the leaves of the fallen tree rustled again, and its branches began to shuffle again, and its twigs began to snap again. *Something* was underneath it.

Up through the branches a horn appeared, with a leaf stuck on to it. Up came an ear, with a little dead twig in it. Up came the face of the Challenging Bull, dusty and dirty and very surprised.

He saw the fallen broken branches, and the jagged trunk where the tree had stood.

Farther away, he saw three smiling faces, Elephant, Goat, and Rhinoceros, watching him.

Out on the plain, at last, he saw Rat.

Rat's little legs were stumping and thumping, and his fat red body was bouncing up and down. He was singing to himself in a joyful little squeak:

'Bull said couldn't, Rat said will.
Rat went quietly down the hill.
Nibble nibble, down fell tree.
But where is Bull? Where *can* he be?'

Elephant, Goat, and Rhinoceros looked at Bull's

face sticking up out of the tree, and they laughed and laughed.

They laughed until they lost their breath.

They laughed until it made them ache.

They laughed until it hurt their ribs.

But Bull did not laugh. He did not think it was funny.

Happy Black Grackle

GRACKLE BIRD sat in a tree by the river, making up poems about her friends. And the trouble was, her friends did not like it.

'Why don't they like it?' Grackle Bird said, and she spoke to a little black fly on a reed:

'Why do my friends think my poems are hateful?
I say what I think, so they ought to be grateful.

271

I'm not just an any-old Poetry Bird.
I rhyme every time with the very best word.
I know what I say and I say what I know,
So why do they histle and bristle me so?
Why do they gruffle and bruffle and say
That if I don't stop it they'll drive me away?'

But Fly had fallen asleep on a reed, so he did not
answer Grackle Bird's questions. Nor did he see little
Archer Fish coming, skimming the water and searching for insects.

Archer Fish said, 'I shall shoot that fly.'

He filled his mouth with drops of water, and swam
up closer to Fly, taking aim. Then he shot the water
out of his mouth, spit-spit-sput, and knocked Fly
backwards.

'I got him,' he gurgled. 'I spit-spit-sput him.'

But Grackle Bird looked down her beak, and said:

'Your game was
Your aim was
To kill little fly.
You shot him
You got him
But why should he die?
He dozed there
Eyes closed there
No one to warn him.
It's bad and
It's sad and
It's sorrow to mourn him.'

Grackle Bird smiled. The poem pleased her. But

Archer Fish splashed the water and said, 'It's ridiculous nonsense! Fly is my friend. He's sitting there smiling. See? On the flower!'

Grackle Bird turned to look at Fly, and Archer Fish filled his mouth with water and aimed at her fine upstanding tail. But Grackle Bird did not stay to be shot at. She flapped unhappily over the jungle.

'I don't understand it,' she said to herself, as she settled down on a juniper tree. '*Why* do they hate my beautiful poems?'

High in a nearby mango tree a little green tailor bird made his nest. First he made a cradle to hold it, from two big mango leaves sewn together. He pecked little holes at the edge of each leaf, and then he made stitches with cobweb thread. Each tiny thread was pulled through the holes and carefully knotted to keep it firm. Then Tailor Bird built his nest in the cradle, a soft little hollow of cotton wool, and tiny feathers, and delicate grass stems. Later, his wife would come, and lay eggs. Then baby birds would be there in the nest, safe and warm in their high-up cradle.

Tailor Bird looked at his nest, and was pleased.

But Grackle Bird looked down her beak and said:

'Bird-wife will come to you; bird-wife will sing.
But watch for the creeping black shadow to spring.
Sun in the morning and sorrow at night.

'Soon you'll have bird-babies, warm in the nest.
But shadow is waiting until you must rest.
Sun in the morning and sorrow at night.

273

'Shadow is on your nest; Cat has come creeping,
Stolen your babies, and bird-wife is weeping.
Sun in the morning and sorrow at night.'

Grackle Bird smiled, and closed her eyes.

Angry green wings beat about her head, and a snapping little voice cried, 'Dirt and feathers! Dirt and
feathers! That's what Grackle Bird nests are made of;
in nasty black holes in old rotten trèe stumps. What
do *you* know about beautiful things?'

Grackle Bird spread her big black wings, and
flapped unhappily over the reed brakes.

'Why?' she said, as she perched on a willow tree.
'Why do they hate my beautiful poems?'

With thudding hooves and sweeping horns, Buffalo
galloped across the plain. Feeling hot, he stopped at
a pool, and rolled about in the smooth grey mud until

it covered him all over. Then he felt cool and re-freshed and contented.

But Grackle Bird looked down her beak, and said:

> 'Buffalo's coat was as black as night,
> Except for his legs, which were snowy white.
> Buffalo rolled in the mud today.
> His coat is dirty, his legs are grey.
> He's spattered
> And tattered
> And grubby
> And scrubby
> And muddy all over from top to toe.
> He's blotted
> And spotted
> And slimy
> And grimy
> And why he must do it I really don't know.
> Tell me, Buffalo. Tell me, at least,
> Why do you do it, Buffalo Beast?'

Buffalo looked at Grackle, and said, 'I shall *not* bother to charge at you. I shall not even bother to snort at you. If you know nothing, then say nothing. You are stupid. Go away.'

Grackle Bird went away to a dark place, where no one could see how unhappy she felt. After a long time, small feet pattered, two little golden eyes gleamed in the darkness.

'Oh!' squeaked a voice. 'What a bird! How strong! Oh, what a tail. How shiny and long!'

And the small feet pattered away again.

'That was a nice little poem,' said Grackle. 'I liked it. *Why* did I like it, I wonder? I know! It was happy, and said nice things.'

Then Grackle Bird knew what was wrong with *her* poems.

She flew very quickly over the jungle, and perched on a tree beside the river. Along came Archer Fish, looking for insects.

Grackle Bird lifted her beak, and said:

> 'The fly on the reed
> Is clever indeed,
> But not as clever as you.
> For *you* can go spit,
> And black fly is hit,
> A wonderful thing to do.'

Archer Fish smiled, and blew a bubble.

'I think that's a beautiful poem,' he said. 'Will you say it again to me sometime, Grackle?'

'Of course,' smiled Grackle. 'But look, here comes Tailor Bird.'

Grackle lifted her beak, and said:

'Tailor Bird's nest is as soft as a cloud,
A tiny grey cloud in a tree.
Bird-wife will come to it happy and proud,
And in that small nest we shall see
Four little bird-babies learning to sing,
Lifting their beaks to the sky.
Clever green Tailor Bird feels like a king.
He's teaching his babies to fly.'

Tailor Bird said, 'So you do know about beautiful things after all. When Bird-wife arrives, will you come to our tree, and tell her your poem? I am sure she would like it.'

'Of course,' said Grackle. 'Of course I will. But here comes Buffalo over the plain.'

Grackle Bird lifted her beak, and said:

'Buffalo Beast comes galloping, galloping,
Dust at his heels.
Fiery hot sun is burning him, burning him,
Weary he feels.

'Buffalo Beast has come to the pool.
Now he's refreshed and contented and cool.
Deep in the comforting mud he lies,
Big old Buffalo Beast is wise.'

Buffalo said, 'So you are not stupid after all.'

277

'No,' said Grackle. 'Not any more. But I certainly think I was before.'

'Before what?' asked Archer Fish.

'Before I knew how to think properly,' said Grackle Bird.

'I said what I thought and the things that I said
Were the very first thoughts that came into my
    head.
Now I say what I think, but I think what I say,
So all of my thinking is better today.'

Grackle Bird's voice was so cheerful and friendly that all the creatures who heard it came to her. Swimming creatures came through the water. Galloping creatures came over the plain. Tree-living creatures came from the jungle. They gathered around with smiles on their faces, while Grackle Bird lifted her beak, and said:

'There are good thoughts and bad thoughts as
    everyone knows.
I'll think of the good thoughts and talk about those.
So the thoughts that I think will be thoughts that
    are kind,
The very best thoughts about things I can find.
    Happy Black Grackle!

'The jungle is big and there's room for us all
To swim and to gallop, to fly and to crawl.
There's plenty of sunshine and plenty of rain
There's river and forest and thicket and plain.
    Happy Black Grackle!

'So come all you creatures that snort and that
    snuffle-o,
Snakes, birds and fishes, and big beasts like Buffalo.
Creep about, fly about, swim about, walk about,
Grackle Bird always finds good things to talk about.
    Happy Black Grackle!'

'Again!' called the creatures. 'Say it again.'
Grackle Bird sat on the branch and smiled. She
looked around at all her friends. Then she said the
poem over again, right from the very beginning.

There are almost a hundred other Young Puffins to choose from, and some of them are described on the following pages.

Some other Young Puffins

RAT SATURDAY
Margaret Nash

Does 'Old Teabag' really live in a damp cellar with rats running up his legs? Joe doesn't believe it, but all the same, he decides to find out. Imagine his surprise when he meets two very friendly, very tame pet rats! It's not long before Joe and his friend Donna discover that tame rats can be a lot of fun.

TWO VILLAGE DINOSAURS
Phyllis Arkle

Two dinosaurs spell double trouble as Dino and Sauro trample their amiable way through the village, causing chaos and confusion on every side! Continues the charming, funny story begun in *The Village Dinosaur*.

ALBERT ON THE FARM
Alison Jezard

Albert and his friend Digger, the koala from Australia, have a wonderful holiday working on a farm. They meet all sorts of people and animals and do lots of exciting things, including milking a cow and learning to make butter.

THE DEAD LETTER BOX
Jan Mark

Louie's friend Glenda moves house and Louie arranges a 'dead' letter box in a book in the library. But Glenda is no letter writer, and the end result is chaos in the library.

CLEVER POLLY AND THE STUPID WOLF
POLLY AND THE WOLF AGAIN
TALES OF POLLY AND THE HUNGRY WOLF
Catherine Storr

The wolf is up to his old trick of trying to catch Polly so that he can gobble her up. He has thought of several new ways of getting her into his clutches, but Polly is too clever to allow herself to be caught by a stupid wolf and she outwits him at every turn.

THE LITTLE GIRL AND THE TINY DOLL
Edward and Aingelda Ardizzone

Living in a supermarket deep-freeze wasn't very nice for the tiny doll, until one day a very special little girl came along and thought of ways to make her happier.

THE NEW RED BIKE

Simon Watson

Sixteen short stories about a lively and logical small boy called Wallace, his nice parents, his daily adventures and occasional disgraces, all told with humour and understanding.

HIDE TILL DAYTIME

Joan Phipson

The two children had been locked into the big department store by mistake at closing time, and whose were those prowling steps they could hear through the dark?

THE ADVENTURES OF SAM PIG
SAM PIG GOES TO THE SEASIDE

Alison Uttley

Collections of stories about Alison Uttley's best-loved creation, Sam Pig, and his farm animal friends.

THE PICTURE PRIZE AND OTHER
STORIES FOR THE VERY YOUNG

Simon Watson

A picture competition in which Wallace gets paint in some very unusual places, an escaped horse which has to be taken home, magic chickens and great, hairy, striped caterpillars are just a few of the exciting things that come into Wallace's life.